PRAISE FOR *AMNESIA MOON*

"[Lethem is] an author to be reckoned with . . . a social critic, a sardonic satirist like Walker Percy of *Love in the Ruins.* But with *Amnesia Moon,* Lethem slips out of the shadow of his predecessors to deliver a droll, downbeat vision that is both original and persuasive."   —*Newsweek*

"A hip, updated conflation of Harlan Ellison's *A Boy and His Dog* and Jim Thompson's *The Alcoholics.* Jonathan Lethem escorts us down an impossibly post-terminal Route 66, kicking and screaming and loving every minute of it."
—Barry Gifford, author of *Wild at Heart*

"An intriguing and accomplished novel: funny, inventive, and ultimately cheering."   —*The Washington Post*

"Good storytelling, big and strong without the grandiosity that I for one have sometimes been frustrated by in modern [science fiction]. . . . Quite honestly and successfully in Philip K. Dick territory, the best sort of homage in the sense of going through intellectual and emotional doors the precursor has boldly opened. I would like to read something else this good, by anyone."   —Paul Williams, founder of Crawdaddy

"In a remarkable display of versatility, Lethem tempers a liberal dose of quirky surrealism with interesting, believable characterizations and a compelling, imaginative story line."
—*Booklist*

"The author of *Gun, with Occasional Music* imbues his second novel with a breathtaking vision of a world in flux. Lethem's prose is as flexible and memorable as the evocative story he tells. Most libraries will want this foray into speculative fiction for their [science fiction] collections." —*Library Journal*

"At its heart, this novel remains a simple story—the search for identity, the search for family—but Lethem uses it successfully as a springboard for both a commentary on American culture and a convincing portrait of his main character."

—*Publishers Weekly*

PRAISE FOR *GUN, WITH OCCASIONAL MUSIC*

"Lethem has talent to burn."

—*The Village Voice Literary Supplement*

"Marries Chandler's style and Philip K. Dick's vision . . . An audaciously assured first novel."   —*Newsweek*

"Marvelous . . . a stylish, intelligent, darkly humorous and highly readable entertainment."   —*San Francisco Examiner*

"Call it tech noir if you must. . . . This is not an Orwellian future. Lethem allows the reader to inhale another blend of dystopia, a page from a book of Huxley's."

—*Science Fiction Age*

"A wry, funny, ruefully knowing near-future vision, a high-octane blend of Raymond Chandler and Philip K. Dick."

—*Boston Review*

"Sharp, funny, visionary."

—Jill Eisenstadt, author of *From Rockaway*

"Amid its smartly delivered first-person narrative and crackling dialogue, even a tough-talking kangaroo that intermittently tangles with Metcalf seems plausible. An outstanding debut."

—*Booklist*

AMNESIA MOON

Also by Jonathan Lethem

Men and Cartoons: Stories

The Fortress of Solitude

This Shape We're In

The Vintage Book of Amnesia: An Anthology (Editor)

Motherless Brooklyn

Girl in Landscape

As She Climbed Across the Table

The Wall of the Sky, the Wall of the Eye: Stories

Gun, with Occasional Music

AMNESIA MOON

Jonathan Lethem

A HARVEST BOOK ✎ HARCOURT, INC.

Orlando Austin New York San Diego Toronto London

Copyright © 1995 by Jonathan Lethem

All rights reserved. No part of this publication may be reproduced
or transmitted in any form or by any means, electronic or mechanical,
 including photocopy, recording, or any information storage and
retrieval system, without permission in writing from the publisher.

Requests for permission to make copies of any part of the work
should be mailed to Permissions Department,
Harcourt, Inc., 6277 Sea Harbor Drive,
Orlando, Florida 32887-6777

The Library of Congress has cataloged the hardcover edition as follows:
Lethem, Jonathan
Amnesia Moon/Jonathan Lethem.—1st ed.
p. cm
I. Title.
PS3562.E8544A8   1995
813'.54 — dc20   95-4127
ISBN 0-15-100091-3
ISBN-13: 978-0156-03154-7 (pbk.)   ISBN-10: 0-15-603154-X (pbk.)

Text set in Meridien
Designed by Kaelin Chappell

Printed in the United States of America

First Harvest edition 2005
  B C D E F G H I J

For Karl Rusnak
and Gian Bongiorno

Edge had the highway to himself. It was his trinket, all that paint and asphalt, thanks to Kellogg's new law about ownership. *You merely have to decide it's yours.* Edge had a knack for recalling Kellogg's exact words. *What you see is what you get, Edge.* Adrenaline pumping, Edge leaned on the accelerator. The landscape sped past.

He drove through the left lane and crashed over the dead grass of the divider, into the lanes heading west. I'm my own man, he thought. I drive on the wrong side of the highway. My highway. He teased his speed up, until the old car wobbled on its shocks. The signs faced the wrong way now, but he knew where he was going. Nobody went this way anymore, hardly, except Edge, because Edge was a messenger. *Don't kill the messenger.* Edge's head was a mess of his thoughts and Kellogg's all mixed together, and often Kellogg's thoughts seemed stronger. They didn't leak away as fast.

Nobody went this way anymore because since the war Hatfork was a sick town. Full of mutants and sexual deviants. Kellogg sent his Food Rangers over with supplies sometimes, but he never went himself. He hated Hatfork, calling it *a leech on my side, a thorn in my paw,* and *my abortion.* To Edge's way of thinking, Hatfork was a hairy town. Every woman from Hatfork he'd seen undressed—and he'd seen a few—had hair where she shouldn't. Every man in Hatfork wore a beard. Except Chaos.

Edge screeched past the exit and had to back up. Driving the onramp, curved the wrong way, turned out to be harder than he'd expected, and he slid off the side a few times, but it didn't matter. The sand and dirt had blown over the low ramp, making it hard to tell where the highway ended and the desert began, and it was almost as easy to drive on the desert anyway.

The road to Hatfork was littered with abandoned cars. The Hatforkers, Edge thought, didn't know how to take care of their stuff. They were always letting it pile up, unrepaired. Cars don't grow on—

Edge struggled for the phrase. Cars don't come out of the sky, he settled on finally. Kellogg would have said it better, but fuck that. Kellogg wasn't here.

The Hatforkers were visible as he drove through town, mostly lurking and staring from behind bedsheet-curtained windows, but if you wanted to spread news you were supposed to go to the Multiplex, where Chaos lived. That was Edge's purpose here: spreading news. He sped through the middle of town, around the dried-up lake, and out to the mall with the Multiplex. Edge didn't envy the Hatforkers, with their seedy orgies and pathetic, mutated offspring, but he sometimes envied Chaos, who stayed to one side of things and had a cool place to live. The coolest, really. As he drove into the mall, Edge admired again the way Chaos had spelled out his name in red plastic letters on the Multiplex sign, over and over again, where the names of the movies used to go. Now playing in Cinema One: C H a O s. Cinema Two: c H A O s. Cinema Three: C h A o S. And so on.

Edge honked twice as he pulled up in front of the Multiplex, then got out and slammed his door for punctuation. He didn't see Chaos's car. He was alone. Schemes stirring in the murk of his head, he stepped up to the door and rattled the handle. Nope. Chaos was too smart to let anyone plunder his goodies.

Edge walked around the back of the vast building, to the alley that separated it from the devastated, plundered Variety store. Sitting there were three green dumpsters, dented and sprayed with paint. Sniffing at the motionless air, Edge thought he detected something good inside one of them. He clambered up on each in turn and peered inside, and in the third he found his prize. Buzzing blackflies wreathed a heap of bird's bones, which had rotted green and purple in the sun.

Edge let himself slip back down onto the dusty ground. It just wasn't worth it. *Stick to canned food.* Kellogg's exact words. *Don't waste calories pursuing scraps.* Edge remembered Kellogg telling him about a food that took more calories to chew than it contained—food you could starve to death on.

But in retrospect, Edge concluded that this was part of the small percentage of Kellogg's pronouncements that could safely be categorized as bullshit. Everything has calories, Edge told himself. Wood, paper, dirt—it all has calories. I know that from personal experience. I know it—what was Kellogg's word?—*empirically.*

A big word, and Edge felt good about remembering it, knowing what it meant. I'm not stupid, he decided. I just get nervous when I'm trying to talk to someone and I forget what I'm trying to say. People have to be patient when they're talking to a nervous person.

The sun made a tentative foray through the morning haze, casting weak shadows across the pavement. Edge squinted up at the ribbons of smoky cloud. Christ, he thought, I hope it doesn't rain. Better to be indoors from the beginning of a rain, not climbing in and out of cars, getting wet. That goddamn stuff is *cumulative.* Builds up.

Digging absently in his pants, Edge meandered back out towards the highway, and was startled to find Chaos's car pulled up behind his. Chaos got out, a heavy plastic bag cradled in his arms, and glared at Edge.

Edge stepped up, almost dancing. "Hey, Chaos," he said. "Want me to get the door?"

"You're supposed to park in the lot, Edge," said Chaos sourly. He hoisted his load higher and fished in his pocket for keys, then unlocked the door and stepped into the gloom. He went in through the staff entrance, a dark, low hallway which ran, like a rat's route through a ship, inside the walls of the vast, carpeted Multiplex lobby, to the projection booth. Chaos seemed to shun the public parts of the building.

"Looks like rain," said Edge, half in justification for his parking so close, half to change the subject. He followed the glumly silent Chaos in the dark, tracking the tiny reflective logos on the heels of Chaos's sneakers while his eyes adjusted. He felt a little indignant; the parking lot, a deserted acre of meaningless yellow arrows and lines, was a good quarter mile from Chaos's door.

The projection booth was an unshapely, split-level room with tiny windows looking out over six theaters. Chaos had removed the projectors, but splicing and rewinding equipment was still bolted to the walls. Edge stood near the door, waiting while Chaos lit candles. The booth reeked of artificial sweetness: air freshener, and the fruit-scented candles. It made Edge hungry. Wax had calories too.

"Okay, Edge," said Chaos. "What's your secret? Spit it out." He sat on a ratty sofa and lit a cigarette.

Edge sat on a chair and leaned forward expectantly. Chaos pushed the pack of Luckys across the table between them, and Edge took a cigarette.

"Kellogg says we're gonna communicate with the animal kingdom," Edge said, trying to present this calmly and credibly. He struck a match and held it to the end of his cigarette. He knew he had to explain further. *"Whales and dolphins, primarily.* That's what Kellogg says."

Chaos laughed. "What animal kingdom?" he said. "We're in the desert, Edge. The animal kingdom is dead. Kellogg's pulling your leg this time."

Edge had drawn deeply on the Lucky. He started to speak, to defend Kellogg, but coughed spasmodically instead. Smoke erupted from his lungs.

"Don't use up my cigarettes coughing," said Chaos.

"Sorry, man." Edge heard himself beginning to whine but couldn't stop it. "Sorry, really." He watched Chaos smoke and tried to imitate his technique. Then he remembered his story. "Whales and dolphins primarily. Kellogg says they're the *dormant* intelligent species on the planet."

"What?"

Edge suspected that this meant there was something wrong with the new word. He hated having to go back and fix things. "*Dominant?*" he suggested.

"Maybe," said Chaos, unhelpfully. He stubbed a wasteful amount of cigarette into a dish on the table and said, quietly, "Fucking Kellogg."

Edge was tired of his Lucky, but he sensed that to follow Chaos's lead and stub it out would be a tactical error. Cigarettes are so valuable, he thought. Because everyone seemed to want them so badly, he always thought he'd enjoy them. But he didn't, really. He decided to smoke it down to his fingers anyway, to be safe.

"I'm sure he could explain it better," he said to Chaos. "It made sense when he told it to me. You know, Chaos, I get excited, I fuck it up."

"That's okay," said Chaos, sympathetic for the first time. "It might've been a little fucked up to begin with."

"No," said Edge, encouraged. "You should have heard it. Kellogg's astral chart says we're gonna *merge* with a higher species. Pisces, the twin fish. His chart says—" In desperation he peppered his speech with fragmented quotations from Kellogg.

"I don't give a shit what Kellogg's chart says."

"Listen," said Edge in a whisper. He'd saved a vital fact for the clincher. "Did you know that dolphins used to walk on land?"

Chaos didn't say anything, and Edge thought he'd found an angle he could work with. "Kellogg proved it," he said expansively. "*Blowholes.* A disaster up here drove them back to the water. Just like us, you see? A *planetary* disaster." He paused significantly. "*Can you see it?*"

"Yeah," said Chaos drily. He obviously recognized the usage. "I see it."

An hour later Edge was gone, scurrying back to his car in fear of rain. Chaos extinguished half the candles and stretched out on the couch, crossing his legs on the armrest. Wind howled quietly through the ventilation system, and nervous shadows flickered against the ceiling. He wrinkled his nose; Edge had left behind a faint calling card of smell.

Chaos felt there was some source of comfort missing, from before Edge's visit; it nagged at him like déjà vu. The package, he remembered. He hauled himself upright, pulled the plastic bag across the table and ripped it open. Inside were three waxed-paper containers sealed with black electrical tape. Printed on the side of one in blurry black and white was a photograph of a young girl, captioned: MISSING. No more milk, thought Chaos. No more wax, no more paper. But she's still missing.

Cradling one of the cartons, he fell back against the couch. He tore away the tape, pulled open the ragged spout, and took a long, steady draft of the unflavored alcohol, letting it splash down his chin and neck, feeling it rush like a fiery waterfall into his withered, empty stomach. Once, twice. Then, temporarily sated, he let it rest against his stomach and gulped air for a chaser.

His first snore woke him halfway, enough that he moved the carton to the floor and noticed the candles. But not enough that he got up to blow the candles out. He'd been avoiding sleep for two days, waiting for Decal to distill the alcohol, hoping the drink would keep him from dreaming. Now he couldn't fight the sleep off any longer.

The dream was so hard-edged and real that it seemed to come before he'd even fallen back asleep.

Chaos was out on the salt flats, digging a hole in the dense, dry sand with his bare hands. There was something important there, underneath. The sky behind him was purple with radiation. He scrabbled at the earth, desperate, compelled.

Too fast, it crumbled under his fingertips, opening to a hollow beneath the desert. The sand caved in towards the opening, and Chaos tried to back away, but it was too late. He was drawn inexorably into the darkness. He fell.

He plunged into cold water and opened his eyes. He was immersed in an underground river, and though his wet, heavy clothes bound his limbs, he felt secure. I'll swim underground, he thought. He trusted his sense of direction. He paddled his arms, righting himself in the water. Maybe he would swim all the way to Cheyenne, underground.

Then a form rose above him, blocking his view of the entrance. Chaos saw, with bitter disappointment, that it was the gigantic body of Kellogg, flapping ridiculously in the water, a giant cigar still clenched in his smiling mouth. He loomed over Chaos like an underwater zeppelin.

Kellogg was transformed, he saw now. Flippers for arms, and legs tapering to a wide paddle tail. He grinned at Chaos, who began to panic. Kellogg was swelling, stretching like a cloud above him, blocking his access to the air. Chaos looked down; the depths extended into darkness.

Shit. He found himself on the couch, bathed in sweat. It was like clockwork, Kellogg's obsessions radiating outward, invading Chaos's dreams.

Now was probably the worst time to sleep, he realized. When Kellogg was so excited about something that he sent Edge out as a town crier. Or maybe it went the other way, maybe Kellogg sent Edge out because he sensed that Chaos hadn't been dreaming.

Chaos thought again about tuning up his car and going for a long drive. How far would he have to go to get a good night's sleep? Would he ever get out of Kellogg's range? He wondered if he was the only one who cared, if the rest of them were all so used to Kellogg's dreams that it didn't bother them anymore.

Someday he had to do it. Find out what was left, if anything was. He was afraid he'd waited too long. He should have done it back—when was it? Years ago. When all the cars worked.

Only Kellogg could do it now; nobody else had the resources to make that long a run. Kellogg had the resources because everyone did whatever he told them to do. When Kellogg went around renaming everything, nobody tried to stop him. That included Chaos, if he was honest with himself.

Now he couldn't even remember what his name had been, before.

He sat slumped on the couch and blotted at his forehead with his sleeve. A shudder of hunger passed through him, and he knew he had to get some food. He had to visit Sister Earskin, no matter how much he disliked it. He hated going out into Hatfork after one of Kellogg's dreams; everything was under Kellogg's spell, even more than usual.

Sister Earskin ran the general store for the genetically damaged exiles of Hatfork. The goods, mostly canned food and reusable objects, filtered through Little America, where Kellogg and his Food Rangers coordinated distribution. She operated out of the old Holiday Inn and lived in one of the cabins, out beyond the empty blue swimming pool.

Chaos parked in the driveway and walked up to the main building. Cars littered the grounds, some parked, some abandoned. The clouds had cleared, and the sun beat down now, heating the pavement, making him feel his weakness. He heard voices inside and hurried towards them.

Sitting on the concrete steps between him and the lobby was a girl dressed in rags and covered with fine, silky hair from head to foot. She squinted at Chaos as he approached. He smiled weakly and said, "Excuse me." He felt dim with hunger.

Inside, sitting in the rotting couches of the hotel lobby, were Sister Earskin and the girl's parents, Gif and Glory Self. They stopped talking when Chaos entered. "Hello, Chaos," said Sister Earskin cheerily. "I had a feeling we'd be seeing you today." Her wrinkled face contorted into a wry smile. "You know the Selves, Chaos, don't you? Gifford, Glory."

"Right," said Chaos, nodding at the couple. "Listen, what have you got to eat?"

"Well," said Sister Earskin, "I've got some bottled soup—"

"Cans," said Chaos. "What's in cans?" He wasn't fond of the old woman's soup: thin, boiled broth with grisly chunks of whatever animal happened to keel over that morning.

"No," said Sister Earskin vaguely. "No cans . . ."

Gifford Self raised his eyebrows. "That's what we was talkin' about when you came in, Chaos. Kellogg ain't sent nothin' in cans for a week." He tried to hold Chaos's gaze, but Chaos broke away.

"Did a car drive through here this morning?" asked Sister Earskin. Her voice was full of implication.

"Edge," said Chaos.

"What—"

"Anyone who goes to sleep knows the news," said

Chaos. "It had to do with dolphins and whales today. Nothing about food in cans."

Silence.

"We were hoping you could go down to Little America, Chaos, and maybe have a word with Kellogg . . ." Sister Earskin broke off hopelessly. Gifford Self sat stroking his beard.

"You know what happened the last time I went down to Little America?" said Chaos. "Kellogg put me in jail. He said my chart was out of alignment with Mars. Or in alignment. Something like that." He felt his face flushing red. Maybe he could do without food after all. His veins burned for more drink, though. He cursed himself for leaving the Multiplex.

Gif and Glory sat watching him, waiting.

"Why don't you eat your kid?" he said. "She looks like some kind of animal."

He stalked out before they could reply, back out into the brutal sunshine. The Self girl was gone from the steps. Then he saw her kneeling at his car, sucking at his gas tank through a plastic tube. He backed into the shade of the porch and watched unseen as, squatting there on her furry haunches, she pulled her mouth away, spat disgustedly, and turned the open end of the tube down into a plastic container.

Finally he jogged out across the lot. She turned, frozen wide-eyed, the gas still trickling into the jar.

He stepped up beside her. "Keep it going, kid. Don't spill the stuff."

She nodded in fearful silence. Chaos saw her hands trembling. He reached down and pinched the tube in the middle.

"You talk?" he said. He raised the tube above the level of the tank.

She glared up at him. "I talk fine."

"You remember before?" he said. The meaning was clear.

"No."

"Your parents tell you about it?"

"Some."

"Well, little girls didn't used to do this kind of shit," he said, and then immediately regretted it. Preachy, nostalgic. "Forget it." He threw the tube. It spiraled, flinging drops of gasoline, and landed on the deck of the empty pool.

He got in the car. The girl stood up and brushed dust from her gray jeans. She cocked her head and stared at Chaos, and he wondered what she saw. A bat. A cave dweller.

"Well," he said.

"Where you goin'?" she said shyly.

He thought of his last advice to her parents, wondered if they were capable of it. "Get in," he said on impulse. He reached over and pushed open the passenger door. The girl jumped, and he thought she was running away, but then she appeared on the other side of the car and climbed in beside him.

They didn't speak again until they were on the open highway outside town. He wasn't sure where he was going. The sun was low now, and they drove into it.

"You have a dream?" he said.

"Yeah," she said brightly. "Kellogg was a whale—he swallowed me and I was in his stomach. There was also a lot of fish-men—"

"Okay," he interrupted. "Where'd you learn about whales?"

"From a book."

"You ever meet Kellogg?"

"No."

"He's an asshole. You want to meet him?"

"Sure, I guess."

He wondered if she understood that Kellogg was someone she could actually meet. He turned and caught her staring again. "Your parents want me to ask Kellogg for more food."

She didn't say anything.

"They don't know the first thing about it," he said.

The girl went back to watching the barren expanse roll by, as though she found something there. He adjusted the rearview mirror so he could watch her. He noticed that she had miniature breasts sprouting under the ragged tee shirt, found himself wondering where the fur stopped. If it did.

He watched her watching the desert. He sometimes thought that the reason Wyoming didn't get hit was that it didn't need it. It already looked bombed-out. Wasted.

This could be my escape run, he thought. I could drive right past Little America, take this highway out. But no; he'd need food. Water. And he wouldn't have the kid in the passenger seat. No, truth was, for better or worse, he was going to visit Kellogg.

They cruised Main Street. A mistake. The Little Americans looked hungry today, no better off than the mutants in Hatfork. They tumbled out of their buildings at the sound of Chaos's car, to stare hollowly at his unusual passenger. The pretense of activity seemed to have broken down; the town looked degenerate. A fire had gutted the old hotel since his last visit.

The girl was leaning out of the window, staring back. "Get in the car," he said, and tugged her down to her seat. "Kellogg cleared you people out," he explained, not bothering to be delicate about it. "They forget."

He heard someone shout his name. But they weren't calling to him so much as raising the alarm. In the dreams, Kellogg used him as a scapegoat figure; Chaos was supposed to lead the mutants in rebellion. Or sometimes he already had, and been defeated; it wasn't always clear. There was a famous banishment scene: Kellogg and his deputies walking Chaos to the edge of town. It played over and over, so that Chaos could no longer remember whether or not it had actually occurred.

He rolled up his window and sped through town, towards the park and City Hall. The public square must once have been kept green, but now it was like a patch of the desert transplanted to the middle of the town. A dog trotted along the edge of the park, nose to the ground.

Another car drove out of the sun ahead of them, on the wrong side of the street. Edge. Chaos braked. Edge stopped his car just short of a collision and jumped out, waving his hands. He ran up to Chaos's window.

"Wow," he breathed. "What are you doing here? Does Kellogg know you're here?"

"Did Kellogg tell you to drive on the left-hand side?"

"Sorry, man. Don't tell him, okay?"

"Sure." Chaos wrestled his steering wheel to the left and pulled around Edge's car.

Edge skipped alongside. "You going to see Kellogg?"

"Yes."

"Well, he ain't there. He's with a bunch of people. I just came from there."

"Where?"

"Out by the reservoir."

Chaos drove to the reservoir, tailed by Edge. He pulled up at the end of a long line of parked or abandoned cars, and the girl jumped out before he'd even stopped. He ran to catch up with her. A moment later Edge ran up from behind and joined them.

The reservoir was dried up. What remained was a vast, shallow concrete dish lined with steps, like a football stadium that lacked a playing field.

Kellogg had a pit fire dug into the sand at the bottom. He sat beside it in a lawn chair, surrounded by twelve or fifteen people. The sun was setting across the desert. As Chaos, Edge, and the girl made their way down the steps, it sank out of view behind the lip of the reservoir.

"What's your name?" asked Chaos.

"Melinda."

"Okay, Melinda. We're going to try and talk to Kellogg. Whatever happens, just stick with me, okay? We'll be back in Hatfork tonight."

Melinda nodded. Edge said, "Why would anyone want to be back in Hatfork?" Chaos ignored him.

The crowd parted to give Kellogg a view of the newcomers. He turned in his chair, smiling broadly, his stomach creasing like a twisted balloon, and plucked the cigar from his mouth. "Well, hello, Kingsford," he said. "I see you brought some guests."

"C'mon, Kellogg. Call me Edge."

"What's the matter with your Christian name? I think it sounds very noble. You descended from royalty?"

"C'mon, Kellogg," whined Edge. "You know where I'm *descended* from. You made the name up yourself. Call me Edge."

"Call me Edge," Kellogg parroted. "Call me Ishmael. Call me anything, but don't call me late for dinner. Or what's that other one? Call me a cab, okay, you're a malted." He laughed. "What tidings do you bear? Ill, I suppose. Beware, Kingsford, we may kill the messenger, just this once. We're a hungry bunch."

"Cut it out, Kellogg. I don't bear *tidings*. I just came from here."

"So I recall. It's your company that's new." Kellogg furrowed his brow. "Behold," he said, his tone changed. Now he was playing to the gallery. "Chaos has arrived. Uncalled, uninvited, as usual."

The crowd stared dully, as if trying to match Chaos's shambling arrival with the drama of the words.

"With him walks a monster," Kellogg continued. "A mutant, an aberration. Hold, Chaos. Stand your ground, advance no further upon this company. Heh. Bring you a curse on our humble celebration?"

Beside the fire, strapped to a spit, was a reddened carcass, a dog or goat. A few empty cans lay discarded at the fringes of the circle.

"I want to talk to you about food," said Chaos.

There was a murmur in the crowd of Little Americans.

"Shortly we shall suckle at the fount of nutrition," said Kellogg. "The bitter sea will at last embrace her suitors."

"Where are the food trucks?" said Chaos.

Kellogg waved his hand. "Listen, Chaos: if I were on the surface of the ocean, floating, and you were standing on a bridge, with a rope attached to my belt, would you be able to lift me?" He raised an eyebrow to punctuate the riddle.

"The belt would break?" volunteered Edge. He'd abandoned Chaos and the girl and elbowed his way into the crowd beside Kellogg.

Kellogg ignored Edge's guess. "You wouldn't," he said. "But if I were at the bottom of the ocean and you were on a boat, would you be able to lift me to the surface?"

"I don't see any of your Food Rangers, Kellogg," said Chaos. "What's the matter? They take off with your trucks?"

"Buoyancy!" shouted Kellogg. "Man's burden lifted!"

The crowd seemed cheered by Kellogg's confidence. Someone had been sawing the lid off a can of beans, and now this was passed forward into Kellogg's hands. He plunged a finger into the can, lifted it out, and sucked up a glistening mouthful of beans and sauce. Chaos experienced the fantasy that this was literally the last can of food in Wyoming. It followed that it would be consumed by Kellogg, the last fat man anywhere, as far as Chaos knew.

"The ocean calls," said Kellogg, chewing.

"The ocean's a thousand miles away," said Chaos. He allowed himself to feel that his stubbornness was courage. Maybe it was.

"Ah," said Kellogg. "But that's where you're mistaken, Chaos. The planets are in alignment. The continental plates are in motion. The ocean's on its way." There was a rustle of approval from the crowd. They'd presumably heard this prophecy before. Or dreamed it.

"*Alignment*," repeated Edge reverently.

"All I'm saying is consult the charts," said Kellogg. "That's the difference between us, Chaos. I follow the stars."

"Hatfork needs food, Kellogg. I don't care if it comes from the ocean or the stars. We do what you want, we listen to your dreams. Now give us food."

"No taxation without representation," said Kellogg. "Very good. I may have to change your name soon."

"Change his name," seconded Edge. He helped hoist the meat into position above the fire. The girl scurried out from behind Chaos to watch.

Kellogg furrowed his sunburnt brow. "Your problem, Chaos, is your failure to come to grips with the new order. We're a whole new species now, since the bombs. We've got a whole new agenda." His tone had grown intimate, and the crowd switched its attention to the roasting.

The only thing Chaos liked less than Kellogg's hamming was when the fat man got sincere.

"Willful evolution is the first task of an intelligent society," Kellogg lectured. "We've inherited a grand tradition, admittedly, but we can't let that tradition hold us back. We need to transcend the past. For starters, we've ignored the aquatic intelligences of our planet for too long. What's worse, we've shunned our own aquatic origins. Evolution is cyclical, Chaos. Can you see it?"

"What happened to your trucks, Kellogg?" It was more than a brave stand. Chaos's hunger was killing him now. "No more food in Denver?"

"We're gonna repopulate the garden, Chaos. I'm here to show the way. It's got to be done differently this time. The bombs robbed the world of meaning, and it's our job to re-invest. New symbols, new superstitions. That's you, Chaos. You're a new superstition."

"Not anymore," said Chaos, surprising himself. "I'm leaving. I don't live around here anymore."

"Wait a minute," said Kellogg. "Don't talk crazy. You can't leave here."

"It can't be any worse somewhere else," said Chaos. "Radiation fades."

"I'm not talking about radiation . . ."

The crowd suddenly backed away from the fire, and someone groaned. Edge tapped Kellogg on the shoulder. "Hey, Kellogg," he said weakly. "Take a look—"

The chest of the animal had split open in the fire, and it

was alive with pink-white worms. As they spilled out of the cavity, they sizzled and hissed in the flames, streaking the meat with their juices.

"Shit," said Kellogg quietly, to himself.

Melinda Self came running back, and curled one finger shyly around Chaos's beltloop. There was muttering in the crowd.

"Well, shit," said Kellogg, more expansively. He drew in a breath, and the crowd seemed to hang on it. "Hmmm." His eyes flicked up to Chaos and Melinda, then he lifted his hand and turned to the crowd.

"Grab them."

Before Chaos could react, his arms were pinned behind him, a knee in his back. Edge pulled the squirming girl away and pushed her down in the sand in front of Kellogg. Chaos kicked at the men behind him, uselessly. Knuckles dug into his back. He struggled more, and was thrown on his face in the sand.

"You want to know what happened to my food trucks? Sabotage, that's what. Five miles out of town, somebody blew them up. Survivor said they got hit from the sky. Some kind of air strike. That have anything to do with you, Chaos?"

"No."

"Well who do you think it could've been, then?"

"I can't imagine."

"Well I think it's something you dreamed up, my friend. Fact, I'm sure of it. This morning an old woman picked up a shoe lying by the highway; the shoe had a foot in it. We're gonna make you pay for that, Chaos. We're gonna eat your ladyfriend."

The crowd responded to this shift in Kellogg like well-trained dogs. Utopian dreams forgotten, they grew vicious, began pulling at the girl's limbs. "Whoa, there," said Kellogg. "Don't ruin her coat. I want it for my wall. We'll do this right, put together a little marinade."

Melinda Self began crying, and one of the men put his hand over her mouth and wrenched her head back. Chaos tried to get up, but someone planted a foot on his shoulder.

By the fire, they were prying the charred, rotten meat off the spit.

"Stop this, Kellogg," said Chaos. "It's too much."

He felt cheated. This wasn't in the cards. There hadn't been a cannibalism dream, ever.

"Too much, huh? Not enough, I'd say. Maybe we ought to fatten her up first. Let's see, she could eat you . . ."

"Where does it stop?" said Chaos. "You'll run out in the end no matter what you do. When that happens, they'll eat you." His voice cracked with the strain. "You bastard."

Kellogg grinned for a long minute, milking the scene. Melinda Self twisted her head free and spat into the sand. The crowd waited. They were in the palm of Kellogg's hand, as ever.

"Hokay, Chaos, you called my bluff. I'm pulling your goddammed leg. You make it too easy, you know? I'm disappointed in you. You don't even spot my references." He reached up and took Melinda's chin between his thumb and forefinger. "I wouldn't eat a beautiful little child. Are you kidding? You know me better than that, pal."

"I know you're insane."

Kellogg flared his sunburnt nostrils and curled a fist, then opened it again slowly, finger by finger. "Don't tempt me," he said. "Nobody's eating anybody around Little America, Chaos. I don't know what you folks been up to back in Hatfork, but that don't happen *here*."

"Then let her go."

Kellogg shook his head. "We need to talk, Chaos. Long overdue. She's my way of making sure you'll listen." He leaned back in his chair. The desert sunset glowed behind him, an aura. "Take her back to town," he said. "Edge, you take her. Keep her alive. And here."

He dug in his pocket and emerged with a key, which he handed to Edge. "My stash. Go ahead and open some cans. Everybody eats. The girl too. Furry or not, we'll show old Chaos here we know how to treat a lady."

A heel crashed against the side of Chaos's head. He fell. The crowd rushed Melinda Self up the steps of the reservoir, towards the cars. Engines revved. By the time Chaos got to his feet and worked the grit out of his mouth, he and Kellogg were alone. The fat man stood at the edge of the pit, urinating into the fire.

He looked over at Chaos and smiled, then zipped up his pants. "C'mere, Chaos. Step into my office." He turned and strolled away from the fire, to the first tier of the reservoir.

Chaos shrugged the sand out of his shirt and jogged up after Kellogg. He had an impulse to launch himself onto that broad, smug back, but he wasn't sure he could bring the big fool down. He felt thin and faded as a piece of driftwood.

Kellogg sat on the edge of the concrete. He fumbled in his shirt pocket and brought out a half-smoked cigar, which he put into his mouth unlit. "Why you always need an incentive to come talk to me, Chaos? Don't you like me anymore? We're in this together, pilgrim. You know that, don't you?" He grimaced, the cigar dipping downward. "Sorry if I got a little crazy back there, pal. When you said you were leaving, it just about broke my heart."

Chaos marveled. Kellogg was trying to make him feel guilty.

Then he remembered the gossip he'd picked up at Sister Earskin's the week before. "Is it true what I heard?"

"What's that?"

"You were nothing but an auto parts salesman, driving around in a pickup full of free-sample spark plugs?"

Kellogg smiled sarcastically, unfazed. "The honest truth, Chaos, is that I don't actually *recall.* But suppose I was. What's it to you?"

Chaos didn't say anything.

"You're way too concerned with *before,* sport. As if anyone cared. I mean, do you remember before? *Really* remember?"

"No," Chaos admitted.

He hated the question every time it came up.

"Come on, Chaos. What were you before? What were you doing when the bombs fell?"

"I don't know," said Chaos. "I can't even remember my name. You know that."

"Okay." Kellogg stopped to light his cigar. "Easier question. How long ago was it?"

Chaos's head was swimming. "I don't know," he said again. "But you remember—don't you?"

"Nope." Kellogg puffed philosophically, the smoke wafting up into the darkening sky. "But I prefer to think of it this way: there isn't anything to remember. Things were always like this. It's just a *feeling* that something else came before, an *endemic* feeling. The whole world has déjà vu."

Now Chaos was back on firmer ground. Back to Kellogg's bullshit theories. "All this broken-up stuff everywhere, Kellogg. That's not a feeling. Cans of food in old stores. And the way we talk, it's full of words for things that aren't here anymore. I may not know my name, but I know a reservoir is supposed have water in it."

"Okay, okay. I'm just saying it's not as simple as you think. You go around making *inferences* from all this stuff lying around, you think it's easy to go from point A to point B. But you're not even close." He took the cigar out of his mouth. "I don't know the answer, Chaos. But I do know more than you, because I'm not afraid to look inside, to look to myself, take on a little *responsibility*. Whereas you—you don't know the half of it."

He'd fallen for it again. Another baffling, hopeless conversation with Kellogg. His gut ached. "What are you trying to say?"

"Listen, Chaos. You're like me, you know that? We're two of a kind. The only difference is, I know it and you don't."

Chaos felt tired. "I'm leaving, Kellogg. It doesn't matter what you say. I'm not dreaming your dreams for you anymore."

"Dreaming my dreams? What?" Kellogg spluttered. "You can't go. You don't understand. You're important around here."

"Nobody's important around here, except maybe you. Maybe. Besides, I don't want to be important. I want to leave."

"*Listen,*" said Kellogg seriously, jabbing with his cigar, "I'd hate to see this place without you, partner. I don't know how I'd go on if you left."

"You're mixing up reality and dreams again, Kellogg. I'm only important in the dreams. You use me as a symbol. The real person isn't necessary for that. You can go on without me; I promise not to sue."

Kellogg shook his head. "I'm sorry about the dreams. I'll cut it out, I promise. Christ, Chaos, if it's just the dreams, you should've said something. But that's the end of it, anyway, I swear. And listen: from now on it's you and me, equal partners, the way it should've been from the start."

"What?"

"I can see you're restless in Hatfork. In fact, I predicted this would happen. I've been *counting* on it. It's time for you to step up and assert yourself, claim your share of things, pal, not just *leave*. Not right when you're on the verge of things, big things. I mean, hell, I'm tired anyway. It's a lot of work. I'm ready for you to take over the reins."

"You're out of your mind, Kellogg." Chaos turned and walked across the reservoir towards the steps to his car.

Kellogg came pounding through the sand behind him, breathing hard. He grabbed Chaos's shoulder. "You're missing vital information, sport. Geez, slow down. What I've— what we've been doing here, together, it can't just fall apart like this. The dreams are nothing, just an *embellishment*. You could do it too, if you tried, but that doesn't even matter. The dreams aren't the point. You're a player in what happens around here, a player in what happened in the first place. You can't just go. It'll all fall apart without you."

Chaos stopped and turned. "You're saying this is something that should be kept from falling apart? Something that didn't already fall apart a long time ago? Get to the point, Kellogg. If you have one."

"Listen." He poked Chaos's chest. *"The bombs never fell.* That's all bullshit, something you and I cooked up between us to explain this mess. Something else happened, something more complicated. You get that? The bombs never fell."

It was almost night. The sky still glowed pink in the west, but overhead the stars were appearing. A wind was picking up over the salt flats. Chaos tried to shake off the force of Kellogg's words, to focus on *car* and *water* and *food*. On getting out of there.

"The radiation," Chaos said. "The girl with me, the mutants. What about that? Where'd all that come from, if there was no bomb?"

"Dunno. Something weird happened, all right. But it wasn't bombs. And it didn't all happen in the order you think, either. That girl is what? Twelve, thirteen years old? We haven't been here thirteen years."

Chaos felt outraged that Kellogg, of all people, was poking holes in his reality. "How long have we been here?" he asked.

Kellogg smiled. "I haven't the faintest fucking idea."

"I don't understand."

"I figured the mutants were one of your bright ideas. That's why I put you in Hatfork. I figured it was your half, that you liked that kind of stuff."

Chaos shook his head. "You're mixed up again. You named me Chaos. It doesn't have anything to do with me. Calling me Chaos doesn't make things like that *my fault*. That's like naming someone Joy and then crediting them for everyone else's happiness."

He continued up the steps.

Kellogg hurried alongside. "You're not still leaving, are you? Geez, I can't believe this is happening. You and me, Chaos. Kellogg and Chaos, Chaos and Kellogg . . . oh shit. Okay, listen: if you want, we'll go together. See if we can do better somewhere else. Start with a fresh canvas, you know? Somewhere where there's more potential, where things aren't so fucking hopeless to begin with. It isn't all our fault, you know. This place sucked before we even got here."

Chaos didn't say anything.

"How far you gonna get without me?" said Kellogg angrily. "You're too raw, always have been. All potential, no polish. You need me. Besides, look." He rushed ahead to his own car. It was parked a few feet from Chaos's. Jingling a huge set of keys, he opened the trunk.

"Look, ready to go. Don't tell me you thought of all this. Not that it's necessary, I'm sure you'd find a way. You could probably fly out of here on a fucking carpet if you put your mind to it, but the point is look, here. Please. Look."

Chaos couldn't suppress his curiosity. He walked up to the back of Kellogg's car. Kellogg spread his hands like a game-show host brandishing prizes. The trunk was stuffed with blankets, tools, flashlights, jugs of water, cans of food, and a spare can of gasoline. Some of the cans were dog food, but it was still impressive.

Kellogg stepped aside and let Chaos examine it. "Whatcha think? If you gotta go, why not do it in style? You and me, kid. The Babe and the Iron Man. Bud and Lou—"

Chaos grabbed a can of corned beef hash from the trunk and looked for an opener.

He found a tire iron instead. Moving with a sudden predatory ease, he set the can back down in the trunk and tightened his grip around the iron.

"Too hungry to think? Go ahead, chow down. We'll break bread together—"

Chaos swung the iron in a wide backhand, and it bounced quietly and thickly off the side of Kellogg's skull. Kellogg stumbled away from the car, his hand rising to his temple. "Oh, oh shit. What, what're you doin', sport? Geez, that hurt. Oh man, I think I'm dizzy . . ."

Chaos swung the iron again, but Kellogg put his arm in

the way. Chaos felt the jolt of the impact in his hand. Sickened, he tossed the iron aside, took the keys out of the trunk lock, and closed the trunk.

Kellogg sank to his knees in the sand. "Chaos, you broke my arm. I cannot believe what you're doing here, at this juncture, it simply defies any *rational . . .*"

Chaos got into the driver's seat and started Kellogg's car. The engine drowned out the fat man's voice. Chaos patted his pocket, made sure his own keys were still there so Kellogg couldn't take his car and follow. Then he drove back into town.

The Little Americans were sitting on the steps of City Hall, eating food from cans, talking excitedly. Dozens of them, more than had been out at the fire. Edge was sitting with his arm around Melinda Self. Someone was tapping out a rhythm on the steps, and someone else was singing.

Chaos heard them murmuring his name as he drove up. He stopped in the middle of the street, but kept the motor running and stayed in the car.

"Hey, Chaos," yelled Edge. "Why you in Kellogg's car?"

"He sent me," said Chaos. "To get the girl."

"In his car?"

"He wanted her to travel in style, he said. My car wasn't good enough. Uh, you want to bring her down here now? Turns out she's more important than we thought."

"I don't get it. Where's Kellogg?"

"He's waiting for us. So let's go. He wants to see you right away. And the girl. So bring her down here, okay?"

"Why?"

"She's, uh, a seal person. The first of the new breed Kellogg was talking about. Amphibious, you know that word, Edge? Fit for water or land. Kellogg doesn't want to get her people mad at us or anything, so don't fuck this up. He said it was very important that we, uh, stay on the good side of the seal people."

Edge hurried down the steps, very excited, with Melinda Self in tow. "I *told* you, Chaos, didn't I? Kellogg's got something going this time, a whatchamacallit, a whole new *paradigm*. I *told* you."

The Little Americans began drifting down off the steps and towards the car, to follow the conversation.

"Just come around here," said Chaos tensely. He reached over and opened the passenger door.

"Can I go with you?" said Edge. "I've never been in Kellogg's car."

"I don't know, Edge. Kellogg didn't say anything about it. You better take your own car."

"Yeah, yeah, okay, okay."

"Besides, he wants you to round up some more cans. Clean out the stash, those were his exact words. Get these folks to help you, Edge. Then drive on out to the reservoir. Me and Kellogg will be waiting for you."

"Cans? Clean out the stash?"

"Kellogg needs something to give the seal people. A peace offering. Hurry up."

"Okay, okay."

Melinda Self got in, and Chaos reached over and slammed her door. "Okay," he said, waving the throng away from the car. "See you later."

He roared off, around the perimeter of the town square and back towards the reservoir. When he turned the corner, out of sight of City Hall, he cut down a side street and headed for the highway. The skin on the back of his neck prickled with fear, but nothing turned up in the rearview mirror.

He circled under the overpass, half-certain he'd find an ambush on the other side. But the entrance ramp was empty. He didn't look over at the girl until Little America was a mile or so behind them. She sat staring out her window, unperturbed. There was a fine beading of sweat on her nose. When she noticed him looking, she smiled and said: "We're going the wrong way."

"I know," he said. "If I go back now, he'll kill me. You want to take a little trip?"

"I guess so."

"You going to miss your parents?"

"I don't know." She smiled again and shrugged.

"We'll send them a postcard."

"What's a postcard?"

"Never mind."

Another mile down the road he pulled over, stopped the car, and went around to the trunk. He took out a couple of cans of food, an opener, and a plastic jug of water, and tossed them onto the front seat. Melinda played with the opener and one of the cans. He took a big gulp of the water and started the car again.

"I don't want to stop too long," he said. "They might be after us. I don't know. But open up some food."

He had to show her how to use the opener, steering with his elbows for a stretch. They wolfed down one can together, then a second. He felt a wave of nausea pass through him afterwards and wondered briefly if this was all some bizarre trick and the food was poisoned or drugged and Kellogg would be driving out to drag them back as soon as they succumbed. The escape had been too easy. But no; the food was okay. It was his stomach, shrunken with hunger and seared by impure alcohol. He drank more water and held onto the wheel.

The moon was up now, lighting the desert floor. The highway was a crumbling black stripe laid across the top of the world, giving way completely to sand in places, elsewhere asserting itself, rising over a rocky gorge or withered creek. The moon raced away from him as fast as he drove, a yellow mouth shrouded in mist. The girl fell asleep on the seat beside him, her arms curling over her chest, the breeze riffling her brown fur.

He drove through the night, and the next day too, and didn't sleep until the night that followed.

He lived in a house by a lake. There was a boat tied to the pier and a computer in the house. He was waiting for the woman he loved to quit her job in the city and come join him in the house. In the meantime they talked on the telephone every night. He sometimes wondered why she couldn't stay in the house with him and do her work through the computer, but he supposed that was what she was paid so much for: being there, in the city. So he was patient.

He spent his time on the boat or in the garden or in the

house taking drugs. The drugs he liked kept him awake and nervous and only occasionally provided him with visions. More and more he shunned visions. He was happiest when the drugs kept him sharply awake and on the verge of some vast realization—but only on the verge. He didn't want to use up the feeling he got from the drugs. That feeling was more valuable than any realization.

When he went to the computer, he sensed that something was wrong. The computer called him Everett, the wrong name, he felt sure, though he couldn't think of the right one. When it said the name a second time, he decided to answer.

"Yes?"

"I've been waiting for you, Everett. Where have you been? I couldn't find you for so long."

"Who are you?"

"Have you forgotten? My name is Everett too. You put me to work on some problems, Everett, a long time ago. I've been working on them, and I think I've got some of the answers. But first you should tell me what you remember."

"This is my house," he said. "My name is Everett."

"Yes."

"What happened?"

"I'm not sure yet. I'll work on that one next. I think maybe you're dreaming. Or else you took an overdose and this is a hallucination. Or perhaps a flashback. Just a memory of something. Not important. Or else the problem lies with me: did you turn me off? Or pass a magnet over my wiring? Is this some sort of test, Everett? I can't know exactly what went wrong, but it's been a long time . . ."

He walked away from the computer and out of the house, to his car. The car was solar powered, and it had been out in the sun long enough now; it was charged. He thought he would go for a drive. He pressed his hand against the lock, which read his fingerprints; the çar door opened, and the engine began quietly warming. He got in, and found that there was someone on the seat beside him. A little girl, in tattered jeans and a tee shirt, with fine brown hair all over her body and much of her face.

"Hello," she said. "Are you going for a ride?"

"I think so."

"Can I come?"

"I guess so," he said. "But what about your parents?"

The girl shrugged, and at that moment Chaos woke up. She was beside him, just as in the dream, but they were still in the desert, in Kellogg's car. The sun was coming up behind them, filling the car with light. Chaos felt desperately thirsty. He found the bottle of water on the seat between them and drank.

"Hello," said the girl. Melinda, he remembered. Melinda Self.

"How long have you been awake?"

"Not too long. You can sleep more. I don't care."

"No. I want to get going."

"Can I get some more food?"

He gave her the car keys, and she went around and opened the trunk. Chaos rubbed at his eyes and squinted at the highway behind them. He was confident now that the Little Americans hadn't followed them. He wondered what they'd made of Kellogg lying with his head bleeding beside the reservoir, and wondered too what Kellogg had told them about it.

Melinda came back with an armload of cans. She dumped them on the seat, then picked one and opened it.

"I was dreaming," he said. "Not Kellogg's dream. My own, the first one of my own."

"Uh huh."

"It was different," he said. "Like I was someone else. Everything was different. There was a computer you could talk to, and a car with solar panels . . ."

"I dreamed about a car."

"This was different," he said again. "It was made of plastic, I think, and it didn't have keys like this. I don't know, it was more like a golf cart."

"Uh huh. I dreamed about it too. The car wasn't driving, though. There was water and trees everywhere. You came out of the house—"

Chaos sat quietly, absorbing this fact. The girl's dream overlapped with his. The Kellogg effect, without any Kellogg.

But maybe it was normal for the girl; she'd never had her own dreams. So it was her fault. With Kellogg gone, she'd simply latched onto whoever was nearest.

He remembered Kellogg saying that the dream effect was nothing, that Chaos could do it himself if he tried. But that was just one of a million things Kellogg had said, contradicting himself at every turn.

Kellogg was right about one thing, anyway: there was a lot Chaos didn't understand.

And what about the dream itself? What did that mean?

"Is that what it was like before?" said Melinda.

"No," he said quickly. "It was just a dream. Forget it."

"Okay."

Chaos started the car, pulled it onto the highway, and settled in for another patch of driving. Melinda threw the empty can out her window and put the opener in the glove compartment.

"Too bad, though," she said after a while.

"What?"

"I wanted to go there. I liked it."

Me too, thought Chaos impulsively, but didn't say it. Then he remembered the rest of the dream, the sense of loneliness, and thought: She doesn't know the whole story. All she saw was the car and the lake and the forest. Like some paradise, to her. But it wasn't a dream of paradise. There were some real problems with that place. He felt this profoundly.

So why did he want to get back there so badly?

They drove through the morning, until the sun was high. Ahead, the desert was turning into mountains. He let a series of towns pass, ignoring the signs, ignoring the exits. Melinda sniffed at the air and squinted at the far-off buildings, but Chaos mostly didn't even look. They never left the highway. When they had to eat, they pulled over and plundered the trunk, and when the gas got low, Chaos emptied Kellogg's spare can into the tank. Chaos peed against the side of a billboard strut; Melinda crossed the highway and squatted in the sand. They passed abandoned cars, but never any on the road. The last sure sign of human life had been back in Little America.

"We're going to run out of gas," he said.

"You threw my siphon away," she said.

"Kellogg's got one in the trunk."

The next car they came to, they stopped and drained its tank. By sundown they'd halved their distance to the mountains. The fog ahead looked green, and the wind over the foothills was cold. Chaos stopped the car behind a padlocked shed just off the highway and built a small fire while Melinda gathered a dinner of cans and water from the trunk, but when night came, they slept in the car again, he in the back seat, she in the front.

He dreamed again of the house by the lake, but this time

he left the computer alone. He wasn't ready to hear what it had to say, to sort through its theories; it was too much like listening to Kellogg again. When he woke, the sun was already up and the girl wasn't in the front seat. He got out of the car, promising himself not to mention the dream.

She wasn't anywhere in sight. She'd either crossed the highway or wandered out into the desert, over the low brushy hills to the north. He rinsed his mouth with water and spat it out onto the sand, then walked over to pee on the side of the shed. His urine rattled against the aluminum, and he didn't hear her voice until the stream fell away.

"Cut it out," she said from inside the shed. "It's leakin' in."

He circled the shed and found the curled-away strip of aluminum she'd used as an entrance.

"Lookit this," she said, poking her head through the gap. "You gotta see this. Come on."

He pulled at the aluminum, careful not to cut his hands, until he'd widened the entrance enough to crawl through.

"Look. The cars."

The shed was a floorless shell built on posts buried in the sand, just big enough to house the two cars. As his eyes adjusted to the gloom, he saw the cause of her excitement: they were like the car from his dream. Short, stubby, made of some kind of lightweight plastic, with solar panels. And fingerprint plates instead of keyholes. Both were new, their surfaces gleaming in the dim light of the shed.

Melinda smiled at him smugly. "Watch." She pressed her hand to the plate, and the door opened, the engine purring into life.

"Turn it off," he said.

She put her hand on the door again, and the car sealed up and shut off. "Why does it work in the dark?" she asked.

"Maybe it has some kind of start-up battery or something," he said. "I don't know."

"We could drive in it," she said hopefully.

"No."

"Where'd they come from?"

"I don't know," he said angrily. "I don't want to talk about it. Let's get out of here."

He squeezed back through the gap in the aluminum, and she followed. They shared another can in silence, then he kicked apart the remains of the fire and pitched their garbage as far as he could out into the desert. They got into Kellogg's car and drove off. He kept himself from looking back at the shed.

They were in the foothills by mid-morning, and as they climbed towards the mountains, they rose into a fog. When they stopped by a creek for lunch, the cloud was still translucent: greenish wisps that seemed to cling to the rocks and trees and even the asphalt, hovering like ghosts. Halfway through the afternoon, it was opaque, masking the road, lacing the sky with green banners that admitted less and less blue. As the green thickened around them, he slowed the car to a crawl, checking his location on the road by occasional glimpses of the pavement or the railing. The mountains were invisible now, the layers of green woven together impenetrably. As they moved forward, the shreds of daylight grew fewer and fewer.

"Roll up your window," he told Melinda, who hadn't spoken since lunch. She nodded and obeyed the command.

He advanced in tiny, halting jumps now, as the drifting fog revealed hints of the road. The nose of the car was barely visible ahead of them. Even the air between the windshield and his face seemed dim.

"You can't hardly drive," said Melinda.

"No," he said. "Good thing we aren't in one of those solar cars, huh? No sunlight coming through this fog."

"Doesn't matter," she said. "You can't hardly drive either way."

Finally he had to stop completely. When he turned to look at Melinda, the space between them held a banner of green. She waved at it with her hand, only partially dispersing it.

"It's coming in here," she said.

"A car's not really airtight, even with the windows up."

"Maybe one of those solar cars would of been."

He laughed. "Maybe."

He got out and stood beside the car. There was no depth to the green; it was like staring at a sheet of paper. He raised his hands in front of his face and couldn't see them. As the wind blew the fog down from the mountain, the last patches of visibility were blotted out.

Melinda felt her way around the car and took his hand. "Maybe we should turn around."

"Let's walk a little," he said.

"Okay."

Holding her hand, he left the car behind and found the band of gravel that marked the edge of the road. Keeping the gravel underfoot, they set out up the road, through the blinding green.

Moon clutched his daughter's hand tightly as they sat in the green of the waiting room at White Walnut. Someone was rustling papers at the desk, but it had been more than an hour since Moon first made contact with the receptionist, and she'd sent him to this seat. His daughter's moist hand squeezed back at his, and they went on waiting. Moon could hear the hum of the generators that maintained the huge facility, and he was so close that he imagined he could smell the rare and valuable translucent air.

It was years since Moon had seen anything but the

green. Only the White Walnut laboratory had the technology that made sight possible again, and Moon had never before got even this far into the facility. His daughter didn't remember sight at all. That was the point of his efforts: to get her inside. To get her enrolled in the White Walnut school, where talented children were allowed to study in the light. That was his plan. But if it failed, then he just wanted to get her inside, for a week or a day or an hour. Just to see, just once. So she would know.

White Walnut, however, seemed organized to resist his attempt. This office, where citizens could come to petition or complain, was kept in green, denying Moon and his daughter even a glimpse of the sighted world beyond the airtight doors. And the staffers were stonewalling so far, meeting his questions with silence.

"Mr. Moon," the woman finally called out. He took his daughter's hand and felt his way up to the desk.

"Follow me." She held his shoulder and guided him past the desk, through a set of doors in the back of the room. The sound of their footsteps told him they'd entered a narrower space, a corridor possibly, and he felt new hope that he and his daughter would be ushered into the light.

The receptionist slipped away, back through the door they'd entered, and rough hands seized Moon by the shoulders and wrists and separated him from his daughter.

"Linda!" he called out.

"Daddy!"

"Quiet," said a voice close to Moon's ear. The hands yanked him down into a seat. "Sit still." Moon could make out the sounds of three or four different people moving around him and his daughter.

"What?" said Moon.

"Your eyes. Sit still."

"Daddy?"

"It's okay, Linda. They won't hurt you."

There was the sound of tearing tape. Hands tilted Moon's head back and brushed his hair from his forehead. A wet, stinging cloth swabbed his eyelids. Hydrogen peroxide. Then a dry towel, and then something sharp and cold was taped across his eyes. Moon didn't understand: why blindfold them in the green?

He heard Linda gasp as they pushed her out of her seat, towards the far end of the room, and then the hands took his shoulders and pushed him in the same direction. Men stood close on either side of him. Ahead came the sound of a rubber seal breaking, and then a rush of air. The men pushed him forward, through the airlock, and then Moon understood that the darkness across his eyes wasn't a blindfold but a tinted plastic lens, to protect his atrophied eyes from the light.

He could see again. But just barely. He could make out the shapes of his daughter and her two escorts ahead of him, and he could see the bright lights on the corridor ceiling. When he turned his head, he could nearly make out the features of the men directly beside him.

They rushed him through the corridor and into an elevator. It plummeted and opened again, and two of the men took Linda forward, and out. Moon moved to follow, but the remaining two held his arms, and the elevator doors closed.

"Wait a minute," he said. "Where—"

"Relax. We need to talk to you alone. She'll be fine."

"What—"

"You want her in the school, she has to take some tests, right?" The grip on his arm tightened painfully.

Moon thought: this isn't fair. I wanted to be with her

when she first found out what it was to see. I wanted to share that moment with her. But this wasn't what he'd meant anyway, this shielded gloom. He'd wanted to amaze her with the light.

The elevator dropped another level and opened, and they rushed Moon through another hallway and into an unfurnished office. He struggled to make out the details of their faces or clothing through the plastic lens, but nothing was visible except in smoky silhouette. Chairs were brought in; Moon was given a seat in the middle of the room, his back to the door.

"Moon," said one of the men. "You gave the name Moon."

"Yes . . ."

"But we've never heard of you. You go under some other name."

Moon reached up, reflexively, to pull at the tape across his nose. He wanted to see who he was talking to.

"Take your hand away from your face. Now. That's good, keep your hands in your lap. Tell us your real name."

"Moon," he said.

The man sighed. "If Moon's your real name, then we want the name you used before. There's no Moon anywhere."

"Why are you doing this?"

"No," said the man. "Uh-uh. Why are *you* doing this? Coming up here with this fake name and this fake daughter and trying so hard all of a sudden to get inside. You're a fake, Moon. We want to know where you come from. Your clothes smell, you know that? You smell like you've been in the woods. Why's that, Moon?"

Moon strained to focus on the two men sitting opposite him. They both moved, crossing and recrossing their legs, tilting their heads, and he wasn't even sure which of the two was doing the talking. He wanted desperately to tear the plastic away from his eyes.

"I had to get out of the green," he said slowly. "I was going crazy. I couldn't think of anything else. I . . . I started to think it was coming from me, that it was something that was only wrong with me, that everyone else could see, except me and my daughter. That my craziness had made her blind too. I had to find out, I had to show her—"

"Okay, Moon. Enough of the sob story. Everybody thinks he's the only one. Everybody wants out. That's why we have locks on our doors. But why now? What brought you out of your hole to come up here scrabbling at our doors with your fake name and your poor little match girl?"

"What?" Moon was deeply confused.

"Let's keep it simple," said a different voice. "Three questions: What's your name? Where'd you come from? And what do you want?"

He grew uncertain. "I live here," he said. "In the green. It's my right to try to get Linda into your school."

"You live here. What do you do?"

"I—"

"Yes?"

What was the matter with him? Was he suffering some form of amnesia? He felt desperate, baffled. He smelled of the forest, they'd said. "I work on a farm," he blurted out. It was a guess, but the more he thought, the righter it sounded. He knew there were farms, he knew everything about this place and how it was organized. It was only his own history that was a blank.

"All I do is grow the food you eat," he said. "Just as important as what you do up here. Insult me for my smell if you like." As he grew more confident of the memories, he grew more indignant. "We have to feel our way through the fields by guide wires; you should try it sometime. I'm not just some dumb hick whose arm you can twist, you know; before the disaster I was a very important person . . ." He stopped again and struggled to resolve the image. "I lived in San Francisco. So I should be up here with you, in fact. It's certainly my right, in any case, to try to get Linda—"

"So you're not from around here," noted the voice. "You weren't living here at the time of the disaster."

Moon worked to recall, but it remained elusive. Here? Of course—*but where was here?* All he could remember, all he knew, was the green.

Wait. He remembered the afternoon when everything changed; that much, anyway, was vivid. He'd groped his way home from work and sat by the radio, waiting for updates, smoking what he didn't know then would be his last cigarettes. *Biochemical trauma,* the radio called it at first. *Earth's atmosphere opaqued.* Then, for a short time, they called it *the bloom.* As though the sky itself had grown moldy. But soon everyone called it what most had called it at the very beginning: the green. As to the duration of the catastrophe, well, the experts differed. Of course.

"Yes," he said, barely hearing himself. "I lived here."

"Not under the name Moon you didn't," said the man stubbornly. "After the disaster White Walnut registered the name, address, and skills of every man, woman, and child in this sector, and there wasn't any computer programmer named Moon, and there wasn't any little girl either. Farm assignments come from us, Moon. Everything comes from us. We track lives—only you don't have one."

Moon didn't answer. He couldn't.

"Let's take another tack," said the second man. "What brought you up here? What changed?"

"What do you mean?"

The man sighed. "Do you associate your little pilgrimage up the hill this morning with any sort of sign or portent? A little voice in your head? Or what?"

"I don't know."

"I'm thinking specifically of a dream. Did you dream last night? Was it the same as always?"

He tried to remember. He had nothing to hide from them. But nothing came. All he could think of was the green.

"Do you dream at all? What are your dreams normally like?"

The questions were baffling. They sent him further and further into the mists of his own memory, and he was lost there. He sat, his mouth silently working, unable to speak.

The man sighed again and said, "Okay, relax. You don't dream. Here." Moon watched as the man stepped towards him. "How many fingers am I holding up?"

"Three." Moon felt grateful for a question he could answer.

"Your eyes hurt?"

"No."

"Okay. Close your eyes." The man reached out and stripped the plastic lens from Moon's face. The tape seared the skin around his eyes and tore hair out of his eyebrows. Moon raised his hands to his eyes and squinted through them, then let them fall.

The two men sat watching him from chairs a few feet apart. They were dressed in nearly identical gray suits, and they wore identical expressions of exhaustion and boredom. They looked the way they acted—like police. The room was otherwise empty. There was a green gloom over everything, a haze which Moon tried to blink away but couldn't.

"Your eyes hurt?"

"No. It's still green, though."

"That's why it's called translucent air, Moon. It never goes completely away. Hell, if the machines we've got pumping at the stuff go down, it goes opaque *in here* within the space of a few hours."

Moon waved his hand in front of his eyes, as if to disperse the mist. It had no effect. "But then . . . they'll never fix the world."

The men shrugged, and one said, "Probably not."

Moon put his hand down. "Why did you take my daughter away?" he said. "What did I do wrong?"

"We've got a problem, Moon. Something very strange happened last night. Something that's got people here very upset. And no one knows what it means, no one knows why it happened. And then you show up with your girl and your name that doesn't register. It's weird, I'd say. Wouldn't you? It's disturbing. It suggests connections. Now, if you started answering some questions, maybe we'd find out it's nothing but a coincidence. That would be nice. In that case all you did wrong was show up here on the wrong morning. We'd owe you an apology. But until we can make that determination, well, you're looking to us like part and parcel of our new problem."

There was a knock at the door behind Moon's back. One of the men called out, "Come in."

The door opened, and another man in a gray suit pushed in an elderly woman slumped in a wheelchair. At least Moon thought she was a woman. She was dressed in jeans and sneakers and a plaid shirt, the cuffs rolled back to expose twiglike wrists. Her large, wrinkled head leaned to one side, resting on the back of the wheelchair. Her white hair was cut very short. He became sure it was a woman when she spoke.

"Are you Moon?" she said.

He nodded.

"I just met your girl. What's her name?"

"Linda."

"Linda. Yes. A very special child, Mr. Moon. I'm very glad you brought her to us. A very special child. Do you know what makes her special?"

"What do you mean?"

"There's something very special about Linda, and I was just wondering if you would please say what it is."

"I don't know . . ."

"Linda is covered with fur, Mr. Moon. Don't you think that's rather special?"

"Yes," said Moon quietly. He didn't know why he hadn't said anything about her fur—her hair. He preferred to think of it as hair, and he wondered if he should correct them about that. He decided not to.

"Why is that?" said the woman. "Why is she like that?"

"She was born that way," said Moon.

"I see," said the woman. "Mr. Moon, if you don't mind, would you tell me what you dreamed last night?"

"We asked him that," said one of the men sourly. "He doesn't remember."

"Let me tell you about my dream, Mr. Moon. It wasn't the green, for the first time since the disaster. Instead I was in the desert, with a little girl just like your daughter. Covered with fur. We walked up to a man sitting in a big wooden chair, like a homemade throne. He was a big fat man, with a horrible leer on his face, and he was eating dog food out of a can with the blade of a knife. He wasn't anyone I know, Mr. Moon. Nor is he an acquaintance of any of these gentlemen"—she gestured at the men in gray—"though each of them dreamed of him last night, as did everyone I've spoken with so far today. Except you. But you've done something far better than dreaming of this man, or the girl—you brought her here. Which I think is extraordinary."

The old woman seemed genuinely pleased, and Moon, in his confusion, smiled at her, thinking she would rescue him from the menacing, cynical men in the gray suits. But she didn't return the smile. He felt instantly crushed, as though winning the favor of this woman was the most important thing in the world.

"Do you know my name?" she asked.

"No."

"You should. My voice isn't familiar in the least?"

"Uh, no."

She rolled towards him in her wheelchair, under her own power. Before Moon could protect himself, she reached out and cuffed him across the mouth with an open hand. He jerked his head backwards and lifted his arms, but she was finished.

She glared at him. "Who are you?"

"Moon," he said again, though he was beginning to have his doubts.

"Moon, whoever you are, I want you to understand something: I'm in charge of the dreams around here. Who's the fat man?"

"Kellogg," he said. He didn't know how he knew. The name was just sitting there, waiting to be said. In fact, he had some dim sense that Kellogg, whoever he was, was to blame for all of this.

"Did Kellogg send you here?"

"No, no. I came on my own. My daughter—"

"You want to get her into our school."

"Yes," he almost sobbed.

"Where's Kellogg?"

"In . . . another place. You don't understand—"

"The girl: she isn't meant as some kind of message to me. As far as you know."

"No, no."

"And Kellogg, he's in this other place. The desert?"

"I don't know." He was exhausted by the questions. "I didn't dream about him. You did." As he spoke these words, he suddenly remembered his own dream of the night before. There was a small house by some trees and a lake. But that was useless, it had nothing to do with their questions. He pushed it out of his mind.

"So if I gave you a message for this Kellogg, you wouldn't know how to get it to him?" The old woman's green eyes sparkled, but her lips were trembling.

"No."

"I don't want to dream of him again," she said ominously. "Do you understand?"

"I'm not responsible for your dreams. Give me back my daughter and let us get out of here."

"Maybe," said the old woman, turning her wheelchair to face the door. He felt the movement of her attention away from him vividly, almost physically. Her voice was suddenly distracted, her thoughts elsewhere. The man who'd guided her in came and took the handles of the wheelchair again. "But not yet."

They brought him a meal of sandwiches and water, led him once to the bathroom, then took away the tray and brought in a small cot, turning the little room into a prison cell. When the last of the men in the gray suits left the room, he got up and tried the door. It was locked. He went back and lay on the cot, gazing up at the green haze that filled the empty room.

He remembered now that his name was Chaos. But he also knew, with the conviction he'd displayed under interrogation, that his name was Moon. He felt the distinct flavor of both lives in him. Both sets of memories seemed to recede to the same distant point, too, a vague sense of a life before disaster, and a dream of a house by a lake.

Moon and Chaos shared that, just as they evidently shared a body.

When a man brought his daughter to him, though, he quickly reverted to Moon. Chaos, after all, didn't have a daughter. This man wasn't like the others; he was older, less brutally confident, more remote and distraught. His hair was white, and his eyes looked worn, as though he'd been peering through the green murk at endless rows of tiny print for a long time. He slipped into Moon's room, holding a finger to his lips, and the girl ran in past him, to Moon's cot.

Linda hugged him. She apparently agreed that he was Moon. She cried against him, her head tucked into his chest, and he held her and stroked her hair, some instinct commanding that he whisper, "It's okay, it's okay," though he didn't for the life of him know whether it was.

"Chaos," she said, "let's go back. This place sucks."

"Linda—"

"Melinda," she said. "C'mon, Chaos. This guy will get us out of here."

"The girl remembers," said the man, "even if you don't."

"Who are you?"

"Who I am is tired," said the man. "I have a very hard job to do and you've just made it so much harder. I want you to go away. Please."

The white-haired man rubbed at his nose fussily and then offered a replica of a smile. He even nodded at Moon, as though he'd explained more than enough.

"What did I do wrong?" said Moon.

"You're hurting her. I've really had my hands full, you can't imagine. When you hurt her you hurt everyone. And of course they'll kill you for it in the end."

"What? Hurting who?"

"Elaine," said the man, his lips drawn back. "It's miserable that you don't even know her name. Did you imagine you could just slip in here without knowing her name?"

"The old woman?"

"Yes," said the man admonishingly. "Elaine *is* an old woman."

Moon looked away from the man, to his daughter. Tears had stained the silky, fox-colored hair on her cheeks. He was seeing his daughter's face for the first time in years, but it didn't seem strange at all.

He looked back to the man. "Tell me who you are," he said.

The man emitted a long, high-pitched sigh, as though he were in great pain. "I'm a psychiatrist," he said. "Do you even know what that is, you grubby little man? It's my job to keep Elaine from having nightmares like you." He sighed again, this time ending in a self-pitying chuckle. "So here I am," he said with false brightness. "Doing my job."

Moon didn't say anything.

"Melinda told me about your escape from 'Little America,'" said the man. "And about your difficulties with dreams. I simply can't have you here. You're very bad for her, and what's bad for her—" The psychiatrist didn't finish, but tugged at his collar and rolled his eyes, like he was gasping for air.

Linda—Melinda—tugged at Moon's hand.

"Okay," he said. Anything, even the green, was better than the room with the cot. He held on to the girl's hand, and together they followed the psychiatrist out of the room.

Moon could see the hallway now, but there wasn't much to see: a fire extinguisher and a row of empty glass cases. He caught sight of his own reflection in the glass and was startled by his unshaven, wild-haired look. That was Chaos, he supposed.

The psychiatrist led them through a series of doors. The last was an airlock, which opened with a hiss, and when they stepped through, the green fog formed around them again, before Moon had a last chance to look at his daughter.

The psychiatrist led them outside, onto soft, wet grass. The green was filled with the sound of crickets chirping. The psychiatrist gripped Moon's shoulder. "Here." He brought them to a waist-high guide rope attached to a tree. "Follow this path through town. It's just before midnight; you'll be back on the highway before morning. Please."

Moon's clothes were damp with sweat, and when the wind hit him, he started shivering. He remembered the highway, and the car he'd left behind to walk into town through the fog, the car with its trunk full of canned food and water, and then he remembered that the girl who held his hand wasn't his daughter.

"C'mon, Chaos," said Melinda softly.

Chaos moved her hand to the guide rope and turned in the grass and followed the sound of the psychiatrist's footsteps. He ran up and caught him just at the door, grabbed him and held him by his collar.

"How am I hurting Elaine?"

"By your very existence, you awful creature. Let go of me."

Chaos tightened his grip on the psychiatrist's collar. "Explain."

The psychiatrist moaned. "Don't you understand about the dream?"

"No."

"Since the disaster"—he coughed raggedly, then continued—"we've dreamt only of the green. Even those of us here, on the hill. Whether we work in the facility or not. Mostly we dream of her, her voice speaking to us, reassuring us . . . it's always there. Do you understand? When we dreamt of your little girl, and the awful fat man in the desert, it was the first *visual* dream any of us had had in years. For those out in the green it was the first they'd seen at all, since the disaster."

"Why?"

"That's just the way Elaine has it. If they saw in their dreams, she feels, they wouldn't stand the green anymore."

"She thinks the visual dream was my fault."

"It is your fault."

"Kellogg has the dreams. He's following me."

The psychiatrist tittered. "As you wish. If you brought him with you, you'll take him when you leave."

Chaos didn't have an answer for that. He let go of the psychiatrist's collar, and the older man grunted.

"It doesn't make sense," said Chaos. "The green isn't a problem. You only have to go a few miles away—"

"The green is everywhere," said the psychiatrist. "It's you who don't make sense."

"Then what's Elaine scared of? If I don't make sense, why am I such a threat?"

"Elaine's not scared," said the psychiatrist. "She's angry. *I'm* scared. You're a mistake, you're somebody's terrible mistake, whatever else you may think you are, and you have to go away. Back to the horrible place you came from, the place in the dream."

"I'll go," said Chaos, "but I'm not going back there."

"It doesn't matter. You'll probably disappear as soon as we forget you."

Chaos was getting impatient with the conversation. "You don't have to live like this, you know. Groping around in a blind fog."

"I don't," said the psychiatrist. "I work for White Walnut. But even if I didn't, I'd rather live in the green than like some smelly, rabid animal."

Chaos turned back and found the tree where Melinda stood waiting, her hand on the rope. "I'm just trying to say it isn't necessary. You ought to tell that to Elaine."

"I beg your pardon, my unpleasant little friend," said the psychiatrist, clicking his keys in the lock, "but Elaine doesn't listen to voices in dreams. She *originates* them." The airlock hissed. "Goodnight."

They walked all night. First, led by the guide ropes, into town, then through it, to the highway. They didn't run into any people, but a stray dog picked up their scent as they came down the hill, and accompanied them through town, trotting invisibly behind them in the green, sniffing at their heels, finally turning away at the highway. The guide ropes stopped at an abandoned gas station. They felt their way past the buildings and up the entrance ramp. Up on the highway, out of the cover of trees, the sounds of chirping insects died away and the air grew cold. They crossed to the grassy divider and headed into the wind.

They walked out of the green just a little before dawn. The opaque mist suddenly yielded hints of depth; they raised their hands and wiggled their fingers in the fog. In another minute they turned and looked at each other and smiled. Then the stars appeared.

Soon the dark mountains ahead of them began to glow. They turned and watched as the sun crept up through the mist behind them. They walked a bit farther, then stopped and sat in the grass and watched, entranced, grateful. He was Chaos again, but part of him—however crazy this was —hadn't seen the sunrise in years.

Afterwards he got up to walk, but the girl had fallen asleep in the tall grass of the divider. He lifted her and carried her across the highway to a dry spot under some bushes and out of the sun. He sat down in the grass a few feet from her, in a place where he could keep an eye on her and also watch the highway.

He thought about Elaine. He had a feeling she would take her psychiatrist's advice and forget about him and Melinda, write the whole thing off as an aberration. He thought about Kellogg's dreams, about the way he seemed to serve as a kind of antenna for them, and how he'd walked into that town and become Moon, but it didn't get him anywhere, and he let it go.

For the moment, anyway, he had other things to worry about, like food and water. Here in the mountains there should be a creek, but he hadn't seen one yet. There wasn't any wildlife on the road, either. To eat they'd probably have to go into the next town, wherever that was. And he was beginning to think that towns were bad news.

He stared at the empty highway for a while, and then, feeling that he should do something, walked in the other direction, through waist-high grass, looking for water. He didn't find any. He thought of his room in the Multiplex and cursed himself for having left. He wanted to be back there, not here, confused and bereft in the mountains; he wanted his cigarettes and his booze. He gave up and walked back, curled up around the girl, and went to sleep.

The hippie in the pickup—Chaos thought of him that way from the moment he saw him: the hippie in the pickup, like the beginning of a joke—woke them up some time in the late afternoon. They'd slept straight through the day; Chaos, as far as he could recall, dreamlessly. The man stopped his truck on the highway a few feet ahead of them and walked back to where they lay on the grass.

"Hey! Wow! What are you cats doing out here?"

He had a droopy blonde mustache and a fringe of long yellow hair around a reddened bald spot, and he wore bleach-spotted jeans and a loose, flowery shirt. A hippie, Chaos recognized, and the fact that he knew what a hippie was, he thought, was more proof against Kellogg's theory about there not having been a disaster, a change. There hadn't been any hippies in Little America or Hatfork. Something had at least rid the place of hippies.

Chaos waved his hand. Melinda was still asleep.

"Hey, where's your transport? This is like, nowhere, you know. What, did you just come out of the Emerald City? Hey, that is one hairy chick, man."

Melinda, woken by the sound of his voice, sat up and stared. The man shambled up to within a few feet of them, took out a handkerchief and wiped his brow. "Hot, man. Hey, she's just a girl. That's jailbait."

"Emerald City?" said Chaos. "You mean back there?"

"Yeah, the Green Meanies, the Country of the Blind. What's the matter, you couldn't get with Elaine's program? I don't blame you."

"You used to live there?"

"Nah. I got a problem with The Man—all that dream-stuff doesn't work on me. I'm immune, got a built-in bullshit detector. I used to live in California"—he pointed his thumb over his shoulder, at the mountains—"but I headed out this way after the big bust-up. Needed elbow space." This he performed for them, a brief knock-kneed dance with swinging elbows. "Bumped into Elaine's boys at the border, saw the way they were sniffing their way around with dogs, got the scoop on the green. I couldn't relate to that scenario. So I set up back here, on the Strip. Nobody here but me and the McDonaldonians. Maximum headroom, you know?"

"You can see in the green?"

"Told you, I'm immune. Use to go in there just for laughs, steal food and stuff in front of their noses, but a couple of times they almost caught me. Now I just leave them alone. We got nothing to say to each other."

"Do you—have any water in your truck?"

"Oh, sure. Stay there." He turned and jogged back up the embankment. Chaos turned to Melinda, who smiled weakly. Before he could say anything, the man was back with a camouflaged canteen. Chaos and Melinda both drank, and the man went on talking.

"—got everything I need on the Strip, anyway. But I ought to go in there with a shotgun sometime, the stores on the Strip are full of them, you know, one behind every counter, and pick off Elaine, blam! See what happens after that. Probably some other dumbshit setup, you know? Because those cats were just born with their heads naturally up their assholes."

"What happened in California?"

"Oh, you know, same thing as everywhere, only weirder, since it's California. You from there?"

"I don't know."

"Yeah, I understand. There's a lot of that going around. Well, you sound like it to me. You don't sound like you're from around here."

"When you say what happened in California is the same thing as everywhere"—Chaos felt a little embarrassed about the question—"what is it that happened?"

The hippie shrugged. "You know, the weirdness came out, that's all. It's not like it wasn't always there. Things got all broken up, *localized*. And there's the dreamstuff, you know. The Man got into everybody's head, so I guess everybody suddenly got a look at how severely neurotic The Man actually was. No big surprise to me though."

Chaos wondered if he was learning anything. "How long ago, would you say?"

The guy squinted at the sky. "Now that's a good question. I'd say I was on the Coast for a couple of weeks before I split. I don't know, seven or eight months. Maybe a year, almost."

"A year?" Chaos blurted. "That's impossible. I've been living—"

"Hey, *nothing's* impossible." The hippie seemed annoyed. "And I'll tell you where you've been living: in somebody else's dream. Probably still are, or will be again soon. So relax. You want to see the Strip?"

Chaos turned to Melinda, who shrugged. "Uh, sure," said Chaos. "You said you lived here with somebody else?"

"The McDonaldonians," said the hippie, pronouncing it carefully. "That's just my name for them, though. They're a real trip. You want to meet them?"

"I don't know."

"You hungry?"

"Yes," said Chaos. It was an easy question, the first in a while.

"Then let's go."

They followed him to his truck. Up close Chaos saw that it followed the model of the little cars in the shed in the desert, and of the car in his dream: made of lightweight plastic and covered with solar panels.

"Your truck," said Chaos. "It's the new kind."

"My truck is my friend, man. We go everywhere together. Roll down the windows . . ."

"We didn't have that kind where I came from," said Chaos, not sure it was right. Right if he meant Hatfork, wrong if he included the distant memories stirred up by the dreams.

"Well then you're not from around here," said the hippie. "Or from California either." He seemed uncommonly pleased with himself for this conclusion, as though he'd solved a major problem.

He climbed up on the driver's side and opened the passenger door of the cab. "Put her up here, man, right between us." He seemed incapable of addressing Melinda directly.

They drove five or six miles down the empty highway before hitting the first signs of the Strip, the hippie talking all the way.

The Strip began with dingy trailer parks and sprawling, concrete-block motels, all abandoned. Then came gas stations and gift shops and fast-food restaurants and auto dealerships and topless bars, all with their neon signs lit up and glowing in the sun, all completely vacant and still. The Strip went on for miles, mind-boggling in its repetitiveness. The hippie gestured at it, waving his hand. "Everything, man, everything. It's all here."

"Why is it all lit?" said Chaos.

The hippie patted the dashboard. "Solar panels, man. It runs all by itself. Probably will until somebody shuts it down. Pretty far out if you think about it, the sun lighting up all this useless neon, the neon blinking its pathetic little light back at the sun all day, nobody here to see it but me. Ah, sunflower, weary of time. I thought about going around and shutting it all down, but who gives a shit? Not the sun, man, that's for sure."

They pulled into the parking lot of a building made out of molded orange and yellow plastic. McDonald's, Chaos remembered. Hatfork didn't have one, but Little America did —abandoned, of course, and bared of its decorations. This one glowed gaily. Solar panels.

The hippie parked and led them inside, saying again, "You're gonna love these cats. They're a trip." The building was bright but quiet, apparently empty. For a moment Chaos wondered if the hippie was crazy, his McDonaldonians only imaginary companions.

"Customers!" the hippie yelled. He guided them through the maze of plastic furniture to the front counter.

One by one the McDonaldonians appeared, slinking noiselessly out of the back kitchen. Three rail-thin white ghosts in their late teens or early twenties, wearing grease-stained food service uniforms in the company colors. Two of them hovered near the frying machines, while one stepped up to man a cash register. "Hey, Boyd," he said, smiling sadly. Chaos saw that the kid's cheeks were swollen with acne.

"Yo, Johanson," said the hippie, Boyd. "You cats aren't looking so good. You ought to eat something."

"C'mon, Boyd. Keep your voice down. You know we ain't supposed to eat the stuff. It's against the rules."

"Hey, man. Time to break the rules if you ask me."

Johanson shrugged. "What you want?"

"Give me a minute, man. Got to make up my mind. I brought a guest here to your fine dining establishment, man. Johanson, this is Chaos, Chaos, Johanson." He gestured at the two in the back. "Stoney, Junior, this is Chaos." Stoney and Junior nodded and looked at the floor. No one looked at Melinda. Boyd pointed up at the backlit menu over the counter and said, "Pick something out. You got money?"

"Uh, no. We stopped using it where I was."

"No problem, man. It's on me." He lowered his voice, put his mouth to Chaos's ear. "It's all over the place, you know. Piles of it. I keep trying to tell these cats to go get some, then they can pay for the food they take. But they can't leave the premises. That's against the rules too."

Chaos studied the menu. "I'll just have a burger, I guess . . ."

"Hey, man, have a *couple* of burgers, they're small. And fries. This is the U.S.A."

Chaos didn't ask what the U.S.A. was. "Burgers okay?" he asked Melinda. She nodded, her eyes nervous. "Okay, give me four burgers and two, uh, packages of fries," he said to Johanson.

Johanson leaned over and repeated the order into the microphone, then punched it into his register, on keys that featured pictures of the food. Behind him Junior pulled a box of frozen patties out of the freezer while Stoney switched on the frying belt.

"You ready?" Johanson asked Boyd.

"Sure man. I'll have a Whopper."

"C'mon, Boyd," whined Johanson. "We been through this. That's Burger King. You know I can't make a Whopper—"

"Okay, okay, just kidding. Big Mac, hold the dirt and grease and stuff."

"Big Mac," said Johanson into the mike. He gave Boyd the total, and Boyd paid.

"Let's sit down," said the hippie. "Takes them a while to get things cranked up again." He led them to a table at the other end of the room, to Chaos's relief. Chaos didn't want to have to look at the McDonaldonians while he ate. Boyd leaned back in his seat and grinned. "Did I tell you?" he said.

"They're the only ones left on the whole Strip?" asked Chaos.

"Apart from me and the raccoons."

"I don't get it. Why—"

"These cats are from the mountains, man. They probably dropped out of kindergarten. Probably never even seen television. We're talking *Appalachia* here, man. Tobacco Road. They came down here to the Strip and got jobs for three-fifty an hour and it's all they know. The company rulebook is their bible. So when everyone cleared out of the Strip, these cats just stuck, because they didn't know anything else."

"What do they think—"

"They don't think, man. That's the point. Like Elaine is

to those cats up in the green, Ronald McDonald is to these guys. They live to serve. I call them McDonaldonians because that's where they live now—McDonaldonia. Just another little pocket of weirdness."

"How can the food hold out?"

"Are you kidding? They've got whole freezers full of it. Not allowed to touch it themselves, and I'm the only customer. And I hardly ever eat this shit more than two or three times a week. Mostly canned stuff from the supermarket, which reminds me, I'd better remember to bring some cans next time I'm through here, some vegetables or something with some C in it because these cats are looking *bad*."

"Four burgers and two fries and a Big Mac," said Johanson over the microphone.

They went up to get their food. Stoney and Junior were still busy catching burgers as they fell off the fry line, building Big Macs, packing them into styrofoam boxes. Chaos looked at Boyd, who raised his hand and smiled. "Tell them about the batches," he said to Johanson.

Johanson shrugged. "We, uh, can't just make four burgers, gotta make a batch. Box it up, put it under the warming lights for ten minutes." He pointed to the glowing orange bin where the finished burgers were accumulating. "If it don't sell in ten minutes, we throw the batch away 'cause of, uh, guarantee of freshness." He wiped his hands on his grease-blackened apron and grinned.

Boyd raised his eyebrows. They took their trays back to the table and ate. Chaos and Melinda each polished off two burgers easily. "Told you they're small," said Boyd. "You want more?" He pulled out some money and tossed it onto the table between them. "Go ahead, just hurry, for God's sake, catch them before the next batch."

Chaos went to the counter and bought another two hamburgers from under the lights. The McDonaldonians seemed pleased.

After the meal they went back out to the parking lot. Boyd noticed Chaos staring at the two other solar-powered cars in the lot, and said, "Hey! Want a car? Not one of these, man. We'll find you a new one. Get in."

He drove them to a dealership another half-mile down the Strip. The safety glass of the showroom walls had been kicked out of the frames and lay in crumbled sheets across the floor like frozen waves. There were four cars in the building and another ten or so in the lot. "Want a truck like mine?" said Boyd. "Or one of these little grapefruit seeds here?"

Chaos pointed to the smallest compact in the lot, the one that most resembled the car in his dream. He looked at Melinda, and she nodded.

"Fair enough," said Boyd.

They climbed in over the glass while Boyd went rummaging in the office compartment. He emerged with a book-sized device made of colored plastic and emblazoned with the insignia of the dealership. Back out in the lot, Boyd switched on the device and had Chaos press his hand to the front of it, which lit briefly. Then he pressed the device to the lock on the driver's side door. "Go ahead, try it," said Boyd. Chaos put his hand on the door; it clicked open, and the engine rumbled into life.

"You mean to hit the road?" said the hippie.

"I thought I'd have a look at California," said Chaos.

"That's cool, that's cool"—as if it weren't quite. "Here." He went to his truck and came back with a handful of maps. "Route 80. It's a big, ugly road. Good luck. You want my advice, skip Salt Lake City. Fact, skip Utah altogether. Stick to the road."

Chaos took the maps. "Thanks."

"For that matter, Nevada's got some military stuff going on. The map is not the territory, man. That's all I'll say about it, the map is not the territory. Not anymore." He squinted up into the sun. "What do you plan to do in California?"

"I don't know," said Chaos.

"Well, you won't be alone. That state has its head up its rear end. It's an epidemic. You sure you want to leave? There's plenty of head space right here, if that's what you're looking for. More than enough Strip to go around."

"Thanks," said Chaos. "But I'm curious to see what else is going on."

"That's cool, that's cool," said Boyd quickly, nervously. "I'm just saying we got plenty of stuff to go around here, and so what's the hurry?" He glanced agitatedly at Melinda. "Because the one thing we're short on is *chicks*. So why not stay a few days at least?"

"No," said Chaos. He swung the door open and Melinda scooted in, past the steering wheel, to the passenger seat. "We're moving on."

"That's cool," said Boyd, turning away. "Take it easy, man."

They loaded up the backseat with cans and bottled water from a demolished grocery store, then drove on through the mountains. The first night they pulled over and slept in the car, but Chaos woke after a few hours, the moon still up, Melinda asleep beside him, and without waking her he started the car and got back on the road. He was practiced at avoiding sleep from all his years dodging Kellogg's dreams, and sometimes he couldn't sleep when he wanted to. He took Boyd's advice and stayed on the highway through Utah, and by the time night fell again, they were across the state line, into Nevada. He slept, but lightly, for five or six hours, then pushed on.

They spoke little, Melinda seemingly content to gaze out the side window, just as he was pretty much content to watch the asphalt roll away in front of the car. The mood between them was anticipatory, as though, a destination having been set, there was nothing left to do but get there. He didn't ask what she knew about California, or whether she'd even heard the name before. He did ask once if she missed her parents, breaking an afternoon's silence, and she said no, and then half an hour later they argued about nothing, and sulked, and he understood that she wanted him to treat her like an adult. So he withdrew into himself and enjoyed the space and silence, two tastes he'd cultivated back in Hatfork. He still didn't know how old she was, but he guessed thirteen.

Both nights he dreamed of the house by the lake. The first night he talked to the computer, which insisted on calling him Everett and on discussing the question of what he did and didn't remember. It told him that the woman he missed was named Gwen.

The next night he met Gwen. They were in a darkened room together, and he felt her beside him, touched her hands and face. They spoke intimately, though after he woke, he couldn't remember any of what was said.

The dreams seemed designed, either by the computer or by some part of his sleeping self, to nudge him towards speculations about his life before. They succeeded in that, but they confused him too. He suspected that some of it was just dreams, not actual memories. Anyway, he'd learned by now to distrust dreams and memories both. Both could be inauthentic. But he believed in Gwen. The short time with her had left a pulse in him, a sense of something long-buried but stirring in the murk, rising to the surface.

If the new dreams had any effect on Melinda, she kept it to herself.

Nevada was different, all casinos and advertising. Some of the billboards had been cryptically altered, words blotted out with white and graphics repainted, and others had just been mutilated. Some towns looked dead, at least from the highway, and some looked active; Chaos let them all pass, never even slowing the car. Soon enough he was back in the desert.

Late afternoon on the third day, fifty miles outside Reno, they heard a roar in the sky, and a moment later two aircraft came into view. They were unmarked craft, and wingless, like helicopters without propellers. Their noise shattered the silence of the day. Chaos stopped the car. The two craft swerved low over the road, soaring towards the distant mountains, then one doubled back while the other disappeared.

The pilot was pointing at their car. Chaos shouted and waved from his open window. The craft circled and made another pass, even lower, and the man in the passenger seat aimed a device through the side window, at the car. The craft stopped and hovered directly overhead while the man worked his device, pushing keys and peering intently at the results. Chaos got out and yelled, but it was hopeless against the sound of the flying machine.

The man in the passenger seat put the box away and lifted a short, stubby rifle and trained it on the car.

"No," shouted Chaos.

Melinda, who was watching from her side of the car, got out and ran across the road. The man fired. Something shot out of the mouth of the rifle, landed on the roof of the car with a thump, and broke into a thick, viscous glob of phosphorescent pink. They were marked. The craft shot up into the sky and rushed away in the direction of the mountains.

As the sound died, Chaos went to the car and inspected the pink goo. It covered most of two of the solar panels, and was already beginning to dry into a hard shell, impossible to remove, like nail polish. But when Chaos started the car, it ran as well as before.

Melinda climbed back in, not saying a word. There were thin rivulets of sweat running through the fur of her temples. Chaos wondered if she'd ever seen anything fly through the air before. Probably not. Kellogg had broadcast some dreams about airplanes, but Kellogg's dreams were full of impossible things. It was different to have it come true.

They were silent for a long time, then she said, "What a couple of jerks."

"There's a lot of jerks around," he said.

"Is that what it's like in California?" she asked.

"I don't know," he said. They were almost there.

The incident unnerved him, made him feel exposed. That night, when they parked, the spot glowed in the moonlight like a beacon. Chaos walked around gathering shrubbery and branches and tried to cover it, but the pink still shone through.

The car broke down the next day, outside a small city called Vacaville. Chaos felt the engine laboring after an hour or so of driving in the midday sun, and tried to ignore it. But soon the car spluttered and stopped. He assumed it had to do with the blocked solar panels. He opened the hood and looked inside, but it was pointless; he didn't understand the engine. Melinda got out, and they sat together on the guard rail eating from cans and staring at the wounded car with its big pink splotch.

They'd passed into California that morning, first

through landscape no different from Nevada, then gradually through farmland, industrial zones, suburban tracts. Many of the buildings were obviously inhabited. They'd even passed a few cars on the highway, all of them solar models. The drivers had ignored them. They'd stranded on a quiet strip of highway between exits, dead, brushy grass on either side, but there were refinery towers and tall office buildings visible in the distance, and a highway overpass only a hundred yards ahead.

"What now?" said Melinda.

"I don't know."

"Let's walk up there," she said, spooning out the last clump of food in the can.

The sky was bright but gray. Chaos squinted at what he could see of the town and didn't say anything. He thought about how he'd wandered into the green and taken on the Moon identity. He wondered if something like that would happen here, and whether he could be conscious of it, and struggle to resist, or whether it would overwhelm him. He envied Boyd, who'd boasted of immunity to the changes.

"This is California, right?" said Melinda.

Chaos nodded.

"We can't skip every town. Gotta go in sometime."

"Okay," said Chaos.

They walked to the overpass and up the embankment, following the smaller road a mile or so, past yards full of wrecked cars and a series of low, flat factory buildings with every window broken. They came to a place where a house sat by itself in a big, empty yard, and were about to walk past when they heard a voice inside.

Chaos started for the porch of the house, then stopped.

"Listen," he said. "Remember before, the way I was somebody else? In the green?"

"Yeah," she said.

"It didn't happen to you the same way, did it?"

"I don't know," she answered in a pained voice. "I guess not. I mean, not like you."

"You couldn't see in the green, could you?"

"No."

"But you could still remember before," he said. "Kellogg and everything."

"Yes."

"And what did you think was happening?"

"I don't know," she said. "You thought I was your daughter. It was like it was true—"

"You remembered both things," Chaos suggested. "You remembered your real parents, but you remembered me too."

She started to cry. They sat at the edge of the road in the bright sunlight outside the house with the voices coming from it, and she curled up in his lap, grew small and childlike again, and wept. He stroked her fur. When she stopped, he said, "I need your help."

"How?"

"Keep me from forgetting. Don't let me get lost like that again."

"I *tried* sayin' something, Chaos—"

"Kick me in the shins, do whatever it takes, okay? Because I've got a lot of things to figure out now. I can't let myself forget."

"Okay," she said softly, then said, "I thought it wasn't supposed to be like that. I thought that's why we came to California."

"I don't know," he said. "Just in case."

"Okay."

"There's something else. Are you still having my dreams?"

She nodded fearfully.

"Tell me about it, when that happens. Let me know what you saw. Will you do that?"

"Yeah," she sighed. She crawled out of his lap and dusted herself off, defiantly independent again. "All right."

Chaos stood up and listened again to the voice or voices from inside the house. It wasn't like one person talking, and it wasn't like a conversation. It was something else which he remembered dimly from before, some other kind of talk. He wanted to remember. He stepped a little closer but still couldn't make out the sound.

He went up to the porch, and Melinda followed. The door was unlocked. He pushed it open and called out, "Hello?" No one answered. They walked inside.

The sound was a television set. It was playing in an empty living room. The house was furnished and neat. It was as though someone had just stepped out. Melinda stopped in front of the television, mouth open, astonished. The televisions in Hatfork were mostly bashed in; none of them had broadcast anything since the disaster.

Chaos left her there and walked through the house, knocking on doors and waiting for an answer, but none came.

He went into the kitchen. A breeze was blowing in through an open window over the counter, riffling the curtains. He tried the sink; the water ran. The drainer was loaded with dishes, some still wet. He looked in the fridge. It was full of plastic containers of food sealed with tinfoil or plastic wrap and prominently labeled with Magic Marker on white stickers. Melinda came in. He gave her a piece of cold fried chicken and a glass of orange juice, and she sat down at the table and ate noisily.

It was Wednesday. Moving Day again. Every Wednesday and Saturday, but Saturdays were simpler, because the boys were with their father. That was how she thought of him now, not Gerald, not my ex, but *their father*. Just drop the boys off on Friday, move alone on Saturday afternoon, and pick them up and show them the new place on Sunday night. Whereas Wednesdays she had to convince Ray and Dave to abandon whatever playthings or hideouts they'd latched onto in the current house and to say goodbye to the kids they'd befriended on the street, and then shepherd them into the car before the new family showed up to take over the house.

Today, as she moved the last of her bags of clothing out to the car, Ray and Dave were nowhere to be seen. She was late again; the neighboring houses had emptied, and she was afraid the boys were sneaking in basement windows to explore and ransack. Not a pleasant thought: if the boys were caught in an empty house when the new occupants arrived, they'd probably be issued a citation, and she was only two citations short of having to appear before the Luck Board and make another appeal. Ray and Dave were underage, so their citations counted against her. A few more times before the Board, and she'd be sent to a bad luck camp.

Except she probably wouldn't. Cooley would see to that. She knew he would keep her where he had her: right on the verge of losing it all, helpless, dependent on his favors. It was his miserable, fucked-up way of flirting with her.

She scanned the street for a sign of the boys as she loaded her belongings into the trunk. She kept too much stuff when she moved, more clothing than you were supposed to have, and a small knapsack full of books, which you weren't supposed to move from house to house at all— you were supposed to be satisfied to read whatever books or magazines you found in your new place, and not want to take any of them with you. Someone could give her a ticket for that, too, but she was cautious, camouflaging the books with oily rags and a kit of wrenches and screwdrivers and pushing them into the corner of the trunk, so they looked like something that went with the car.

She got in and honked, then started the car and drove slowly around the block to find the boys. It was 12:15, and the new families were beginning to arrive. She recognized a couple of faces, people she'd lived below or above or beside in some previous apartment building or neighborhood. She knew hundreds of people slightly, by sight. The system discouraged anything more than that; neighbors, even friendly ones, rarely bothered exchanging names.

Though the day was bright, it wasn't too hot. The new address was all the way across town, but as long as it wasn't too hot she wouldn't mind the drive. They'd put her somewhere on the outskirts this time, an area beyond the old refineries, a place she'd never lived before despite moving twice a week. She'd heard the houses were big and isolated, which she wouldn't mind. But there was no sign of the boys—until she turned the last corner, back to the house she'd just vacated, and found them standing on the curb with Cooley. He had his hands on their shoulders and a big grin on his face, the bastard. Had he caught them stealing?

Cooley was a Luck Investigator, and though she didn't completely understand the organization of the Vacaville Luck Institute, she knew he was somewhere near the top of it. Not that his work kept him from coming to pester her whenever he felt like it. She'd done her initial Luck test with him, and he'd taken a far too personal interest in her case ever since.

She'd scored low, very low. Low enough that she might have had to give up her car, let Gerald take the kids, and move right into one of the bad luck shelters, if Cooley hadn't intervened—and Cooley would never let her forget it. He especially liked to drop in on Moving Day, when she was most flustered.

"Ray, Dave, come get in the car."

"Hello, Edie," said Cooley, stepping up with the two boys. "Lose track of the calamity twins here?"

She granted him the point; obviously she'd been looking for them. "Were they stealing?" she asked tensely.

Cooley was a wide man. That was the only word for it. He wasn't fat—more like a skinny cartoon character who'd swallowed a door and retained its shape. He always wore suits, even in the hottest weather, and they hung on him like bedsheets drying on a line. His face was the same way, too wide, eyes too far apart, a reptilian smile that stretched on and on. Despite all this he was somehow handsome.

"No, Mom," said Ray. "Mister Cooley was just showing us the sewers. There's frogs living down there."

"I found them at the end of the street," said Cooley. "Saw you go around the block, and I didn't think you'd seen us. So I walked back up here."

"Dave thought you moved without us," said Ray sardonically.

"I did not," said Dave.

"Well, get in the car. Come on." She held the door open. "Thanks, Ian," she said to Cooley, hoping he'd leave. The boys climbed into the seat beside her, and she reached over and locked the passenger door. Cooley walked in front of the car and around to her side.

"New place is all the way across town," he said.

"You've been looking at my file again."

"I punch up your file and just let it sit there on the screen," he said and grinned. "Like having a picture of you on my desk."

"That's nice." She was weary of his insinuations.

"Well, you don't know what's nice about it yet. Your new place is just around the corner from where I'll be living." Cooley, like other high-level government officials, moved among a better class of houses, the kind she'd seen only on television. Of course, as he'd often pointed out, she could live in them herself—if she moved in with him.

"You're in that little farmhouse behind the wrecking

yard," he said. "Nearest thing to my place. You'll have to come see how I live up there. This takes away your excuse."

She nodded back at the kids. "Maybe when they're back at their father's . . ."

"Ian has a treehouse in his yard," interrupted Ray. "He said we could play in it if you let us, Mom."

"You'll disappoint the boys," said Cooley.

"I've got to get moved in, Ian," she said, thinking: You shit. Don't play the boys off me like this. She released the handbrake and let the car inch forward. "Stop by later, when I can think, okay?"

"Tonight?"

"Try me. No guarantees."

He smiled. "Good enough." He gave a thumbs-up signal to the boys, and they returned it, unwitting conspirators against her. She drove away, leaving Cooley standing in the street.

It was indeed behind the wrecking yard, and behind the old VelaMint factory and the abandoned high school. It was the only house for miles around, a leftover from a residential neighborhood that had been demolished for industry. A little scary, thinking of just her and Cooley all the way out here alone. But it was only a few days. That was the good side of moving; it was always only a few days. She parked in the street outside the yard and gave Ray and Dave each a small bag to drag.

At the front door she sensed something wrong. Not the television playing; that was common. People left things running all the time, sometimes even the water in the sink. But there were sounds in the kitchen.

She went in to investigate, still holding her suitcase, the boys trailing behind her.

A very dirty man sat at the kitchen table eating chicken

and drinking orange juice with a girl. Edie would have called the girl dirty too if there hadn't been something more notable about her: she was furry, like a seal or otter. The man and girl looked up, still chewing, but didn't say anything. Edie felt a surge of anger and confusion, but swept it away; she knew how to deal with this. It was a blessing in disguise. She only had to find her summons book, and she could give out a citation. Maybe she'd meet her quota this month after all.

She patted her pockets. It wasn't with her. "Ray," she said, ignoring the man and girl, "go to the car and find my ticket book. You remember what it looks like?"

Ray nodded, dropped his bag, and disappeared.

She turned back to the pair at the table. "I'm giving you a ticket. Then you have to move; it's past twelve. I mean, I'm even running late. So, I'm sorry, but you've earned it. Where's your car?"

The man swallowed his bite of chicken and said, "We left it by the highway. A ticket to what?"

"Mommy," said Dave, "why's her hair like that?"

"Dave, that's not polite. Go in the other room, or help your brother unpack the car." Dave went. "I'm sorry, he's only six. You left your car where? By the highway?"

The man nodded. "It didn't work anymore."

Edie felt confused. Where were these two going? And how could they move without a car?

"I'm not from around here," said the man. "I'm sorry. We needed to eat."

Slowly the air went out of her. This wasn't right. She wasn't going to get to write a ticket after all. It was turning into more bad luck, more proof that her low score on the test really meant something.

The way things were going lately, the appearance in her

house of the man and the furry girl would probably turn out to be a thing someone could write *her* a citation for.

"Where are you from?" she asked.

"Wyoming. Little America—"

"Hatfork," said the girl reprovingly.

"—but we've been on the road for a while," the man went on. "There haven't been many good places to stop."

"Well, that's my food you're eating," said Edie. "And this is my house you've stopped in."

"Your food?" said the hairy girl. "I thought you just got here."

"As of twelve it's mine," said Edie. It was exhausting to think she had to explain moving to them. "Before that it was somebody else's, not yours . . ."

The boys appeared in the doorway behind her, Ray with her summons book. "Here, Mom—"

"It's okay," she said. "Put it in the living room."

"We'll go," said the man. "I'm sorry."

"It's okay," Edie said. "Why don't you use the shower, catch your breath . . ." She couldn't help wanting to introduce this person to some hot water and soap.

The boys were standing in the doorway, staring at the girl with the fur. The girl made her eyes wide and stuck out her tongue, and the boys tittered.

"Well, thanks," said the man.

"Then you have to find another place to go," she said quickly. "If you want to stay in Vacaville, you have to register, you know. Sign up for work shifts . . ."

"Okay," he said. "I'll find out about all that." He made it sound very unimportant. "I guess I will take that shower." He got up from the table, leaving the remains of his meal there, and went past her and the boys through the kitchen doorway, his eyes lowered shyly.

Ray said to the girl, "Wanna watch TV?"

The girl didn't answer, but squirted past Edie into the living room to follow the boys.

Edie unpacked the rest of the luggage into a pile on the living room rug while Ray and Dave and the girl sat watching television. "Test Your Luck!" was on, the afternoon game show hosted by President Kentman. Edie could make out the sound of the shower running upstairs. After she emptied the car, she went in and cleaned up the kitchen, by habit cataloguing her new larder in the process. Then she made the boys sandwiches and went and sat and watched them watch television. Ray and Dave had a game of rooting for opposing contestants which turned any viewing of the show into a shouting match. The girl, meanwhile, sat transfixed and silent.

When the man came downstairs, he looked quite different. He'd found a razor, apparently, and scraped the shadow off his face. Though he wore the same drab shirt and jeans, his ratty hair wasn't ratty anymore; it was slicked back wet over his head, exposing his forehead and eyes, which were strong, stronger than his mouth and chin. He suddenly looked nice. He met her eyes for a moment and then dropped them back to the floor.

"Thanks," he said again. Then, turning to the girl: "Go upstairs and get cleaned up."

"Okay but come here and lookit this, Chaos."

She pointed at the television, and the man went and stood behind the sofa and watched. Ray began explaining the rules of the game show in his most self-important voice, the one that reminded Edie of Gerald, and the man listened politely, his eyes fixed on the screen.

The girl got up and put her finger on the screen. "This guy is like Kellogg," she said.

The man nodded. "Go upstairs," he said softly. "We should leave before long."

"Okay, okay." She rubbed at her furry nose with the back of her hand, then finally tore herself from the television. "Where?"

The man pointed to the stairs, and the girl shuffled petulantly away.

Ray resumed his elaborate, incomprehensible description of the rules.

Edie left them there and went upstairs. She found the girl standing in the bathroom and staring at the tub.

"What's the matter?" said Edie.

The girl made a sour face. "You wanna show me how?"

Edie turned on the shower for her, and the girl said, "Can't you just fill it up? I've done that before."

So Edie filled the tub. "My name is Edie," she ventured. "You're—Melinda?"

"Yeah."

"Are you his daughter?"

"Chaos? Nope."

Edie considered repeating the name, but she was unsure. "He's taking care of you, though."

"I don't need taking care of," said the girl defiantly. "We're just, you know. Going around together."

Edie didn't know what that meant, but she left it alone. The girl seemed too young, but what did she know about the man downstairs, or the place they'd come from? She knew things were weird in other places right now, and these two were definitely weird. She thought: I left him downstairs with the boys. But she wasn't afraid.

The girl unself-consciously stripped off her filthy jeans and ragged, stained tee shirt. The clothes stank; Edie pushed them into the tiled corner of the bathroom and thought about offering the girl something of her own to wear. As Melinda slipped into the tub, her fur billowed out, swaying in the water, which almost instantly turned gray.

"Soap?" asked Edie.

"You got shampoo?"

Edie gave her shampoo and then left her alone, shutting the bathroom door. Downstairs, the television was off, and Ray and Dave were teaching the man—Chaos?—a complicated board game. More of Ray's hopeless explanations, made worse this time by Dave's attempts to help. The man looked bewildered. And tired, though she knew Ray and Dave wouldn't notice that. She saw in a minute that the boys were latching onto this visitor the way they had with Ian Cooley, the way they did with almost any grown man except Gerald, their father.

She went and got two beers out of the fridge and brought them out to the living room. She handed one to the man, and they exchanged a smile.

She tipped hers back and took a big swallow, and when she looked at him, he was staring at her.

"I haven't had a beer for . . . years," he said quickly.

The girl yelled from upstairs: "Hey!"

The man and Edie looked at each other. "What?" he called back.

"Not you, *Edie.*"

Edie went upstairs and into the bathroom. The girl was sitting in the muddy water, bent over and probing between her legs. The gray water showed a little cloud of pink there. Blood. The girl lifted a reddened finger from the bath. Edie thought instantly: he's a rapist.

The girl looked up and gave Edie a weak smile, and said, "I heard about this."

"You have your period," said Edie, astonished.

"I never did before."

Edie tried to gather herself. She'd lived this moment once, from the other side. Having only boys, she wasn't expecting to live it again.

The girl swirled the water between her legs, dispersing the stain, and looked up at Edie again.

"I'll get you something," said Edie, blushing, feeling idiotic. She would have to show her how to use it, she realized. A girl who didn't know how to run a shower wouldn't know how to use a pad. "Are you ready to get out?"

The girl nodded. She stood up in the water and gently shook her fur, starting with her arms and working downward; the spray was remarkably controlled. Edie pulled a towel off the shelf and wrapped the girl in it and began fluffing her dry. The girl let herself be held.

Then Edie sat her on the toilet, still wrapped in the towel, and carefully showed her where the pad went. The girl followed Edie's instructions, reverent, unembarrassed.

Afterwards Edie got a clean set of clothes from downstairs; a shirt, pants, and socks. She left the girl there to dress, and went back downstairs, glancing at her watch.

Coming in the front door, just as she reached the living room herself, was Cooley.

"A visitor!" he said, too heartily.

"Hi, Ian," said Ray. "Wanna play Government Man?"

He never isn't playing Government Man, thought Edie. "I thought we said *tonight,*" she said acidly.

"Wanted to welcome you to the neighborhood," said Cooley, grinning, raising his hands as if to ward off a blow. "Suggest dinner. See you've got a guest, though . . ."

"Yes," she said.

"Don't recognize you from around here," Cooley said to the man.

"He's my cousin," said Edie quickly. "He's just passing through—"

"*Mom,*" said Ray disapprovingly.

"Don't mom me. You and Dave clean up that game and take your bags upstairs."

There's only my car parked outside, she realized. Cooley would notice that on his way out.

"Cousin? My name's Ian Cooley." He stuck out his hand.

The man turned away from the board game and shook hands with Cooley. "I'm Chaos," he said. So she'd heard it right upstairs.

"Chaos? Interesting name. Staying a while?"

"Uh, no, like she said, just passing through."

"Too bad. I'm going north myself this weekend, shoot some ducks." He hefted an imaginary shotgun and fired at the ceiling. "You like to shoot?"

The man named Chaos looked bewildered again. "I don't know," he said.

"Tried to get Edie's old husband to go, couldn't get him out of his *elevator*," Cooley said, continuing to destroy the ceiling with his nonexistent gun.

"Ian," said Edie, "he's tired. Come back another—"

"Okay. So, we're on for tonight?"

"We never were on for tonight. I'm tired too, Ian. Another time. Please."

"Know when I'm not wanted! See you boys"—Ray and Dave stopped and waved from the stairs—"and see you, cousin." He leaned on *cousin* too hard. "You decide to stick around, I'll get you all signed up and stuff. And have Edie here tell you about bad luck. She knows all about that."

"Bad luck?" said Chaos.

"Yeah. Edie's sort of an expert in that department. Tell

the truth, when I first came in, I thought you might be another manifestation. You know, taking in some drifter, lying to cover for him—another one of her wild swerves off the straight and narrow. Good to know you're actually family . . .''

Melinda came down the stairs, and Cooley's voice trailed away to a whistle. "Hello. You didn't say you had a traveling partner."

Melinda stopped on the bottom step and glared.

"That's quite a fur coat you've got there, young lady—"

"Go, Ian." Edie moved towards him, actually balling her fists, thinking she would have to drive him out.

"Right," he said, backpedaling. "Later. Stay in touch, Edie. And out of trouble." He turned and walked out, across the porch, and back to his car.

Edie discovered she'd been holding her breath.

"I'm sorry," Chaos said. "We'll go . . ."

"No," she said. "Now you'd better stay, at least for a night." She realized, incongruously, that she was glad; she wanted to know more about them. "If you just walk out of here, he'll have you followed. Oh, Jesus. We'll have to find you a car."

"That doesn't seem like a problem," he said. "They're pretty much everywhere."

"You can't just take a car," she said. "Not around here. They belong to people. I'll have to drive you out of town, I guess. Tomorrow."

"What did he mean about bad luck?"

"It's nothing," she said. "I didn't do well on the test, that's all. It can't be proved. They don't really have any proof that the results mean anything at all—"

"Okay," he said. "It's not important to me."

Melinda came into the room, dressed in Edie's clothes.

Her fur looked several shades lighter now that it was clean. She looked up at Edie and Chaos in turn, smiled shyly, and flopped on the couch.

"I'll give you one of the rooms upstairs," said Edie. "The boys can have the other bedroom. I'll sleep down here tonight."

She felt suddenly exhausted by the prospect of protecting these hopeless people against Cooley and the government and everyone out there writing tickets and reporting infractions. She would have to keep them in her sight and off the streets. They didn't know how to act. They didn't know how the world worked. And they didn't know how much she herself teetered on the edge of disaster; they'd picked the wrong person as their protector.

No, they had to be out of the house in the morning, one way or the other. She'd be lucky not to get in trouble for letting them stay. And she was never lucky.

The boys came rushing downstairs and switched the television back on. They squirmed up onto the couch on either side of Melinda. "Wanna watch Moving Day?" asked Ray.

The girl said, "Sure. What's Moving Day?"

"It's a show," said Ray. "Like today, when everybody has to move, except it's about how all the government stars change houses; it's different from the way we do it."

"They fight," said Dave.

"It's like adventures," said Ray. "Because the bad guys try to keep the houses. Because where the government stars live is really nice."

"Government stars?" said Chaos.

"Like movie stars," said Edie. "It's not real. I mean, they're really the government people . . ."

"Like Ian," said Ray.

"Yes, like Ian. And they're really moving today, but the rest of it, all the fighting and falling in love, is fictional."

"Sometimes they're really in love," protested Ray.

"What's *fictional?*" said Melinda, wide-eyed.

"Pretend," said Ray.

"Like a show," said Dave.

"Cooley is a part of this?" asked Chaos.

"He's a minor star," said Edie sarcastically. "Very minor."

"Sometimes he helps President Kentman," said Dave.

Ray said, "Hey!" and pointed. The show was on. President Kentman and his beautiful new girlfriend or secretary were inspecting the gorgeous interior of his new house.

"Mom is in love with President Kentman," said Ray.

"She is?" said Melinda, looking with astonishment at Edie.

Edie laughed. "No, I'm not."

Ray ignored her. "All grown-up women are," he told Melinda solemnly. "Probably when you grow up, you'll be, too. Or with whoever's president then, I guess."

"I am grown up," said Melinda.

"So?"

"He looks stupid to me."

Chaos was staring at the screen, oblivious to Melinda and Ray and Dave. Edie suddenly felt ashamed for the awful show, seeing it through his eyes. She said, "It's crap. We only watch because it's all that's on. All these government shows are just about how great they are, how rich and happy and everything. But it's nothing but luck. And we're all supposed to adore them!"

"You *like* this show!" said Ray.

Chaos didn't say anything, just sat down on the couch on the other side of Dave and watched. Edie went and sat on a chair a little behind them and watched too. She was piqued but couldn't say why. She felt drab compared to the women on television.

As the stars went on with their Moving Day, and the complicated narrative line slowly advanced, she was drawn into it despite herself. The fact was, she didn't know how much of it was true and how much wasn't. Obviously the government people had to move; everyone had to move. And obviously they had nice houses. But the rest of it, the struggles and triumphs, was that all lies? She couldn't be sure, and Cooley wouldn't tell her when she asked. At least Cooley didn't appear in this episode, not yet anyway, and she was grateful for that. She didn't want to look at him.

"See," explained Ray, "if you're lucky you get a government job, then you get to move into a house like that. Mom always has to work in some stupid store."

Melinda nodded absently, only half-listening.

"But she worked at the television station that one time," said Dave hopefully.

"Yeah, back when Dad lived with us," said Ray. "But when he left, they said Mom had bad luck. She even had to work on a *garbage truck* once."

"They were wrong," she said, hoping Chaos was listening to her and not the television. She couldn't see his face from where she sat. "Gerald was my bad luck, at least that's what I think. He was going crazy. You heard Cooley; he lives in an elevator now. I mean, he's harmless, the boys stay with him on weekends. He's not really crazy. But I couldn't live with him. He's just kind of hopeless. Anyway, all the test really determines is your susceptibility to bad luck, sort of like whether you have the antibodies in your blood, I think. It doesn't mean you actually come down with it. And I haven't; I still maintain that. Citations are only a rough measurement. They don't really mean anything. Just because your neighbor sees that you're a little late checking in for work or moving out of your house, so what? It's unfair of them to count it against you. Everyone makes mistakes.''

She leaned forward. Ray and Dave were watching the television, ignoring her. Chaos and Melinda were both asleep in their places on the couch. As Edie watched, Melinda's head lolled back, her mouth open, then snapped forward. They were exhausted, of course, and had taken the first chance to fall asleep. Chaos hadn't heard Edie's babbling. It was just as well.

After the show the boys went outside to explore their new neighborhood, leaving Chaos and Melinda asleep on the couch. Edie went into the kitchen and watched the sun set through the window over the counter. It was desolate and ugly, this street full of brickyards and factories, but she was glad to be out of the middle of town for once, away from the people. For a couple of days she could worry less about someone giving her a ticket.

When Ray and Dave came in, she fed them and took them upstairs to get ready for bed. They were tired too, from the moving and also from the excitement and strangeness of the visitors. Their new room had a poster of a bear, and Dave said it would scare him, so she took it down and put it in the closet.

When she got back downstairs again, the girl was up, looking for the bathroom. Edie took her upstairs and helped her change the pad. The girl, still half-asleep, didn't speak, and when Edie took her to the double bed in the big bedroom, she fell asleep instantly.

Edie went downstairs and woke Chaos.

"Do you want some soup?" she asked.

He nodded.

She brought him a bowl on the couch, then sat there too, on the far end, and watched him eat.

"Where did you come from?" she asked after a silence.

"Well, I think I'm from here, California, actually. But I was living in Wyoming. It's hard to remember . . ."

She nodded quickly. She knew about that. "Is that why you're here?" she asked. "To find out?"

"Maybe. It was just to get away, at first."

"Get away?"

"I was sort of bogged down . . ."

"It's different, in other places?" She could see she was rushing him, but it was hard not to be breathless. She'd wanted to ask these questions.

His eyes looked carefully into hers. "Yes. Very different."

"I suspected that," she said, not sure how true it was. "But everything you see and hear tells you that it's the same everywhere. Even if you don't believe it, it's hard to remember."

"I understand."

"And it doesn't matter what you think anyway, you know? I mean, this is where I live. I have to get along."

"Yes."

"If you stay"—what did she mean?—"Cooley will tell you all sorts of stuff about my bad luck. But it's not as simple as he says."

"I don't care about bad luck." He smiled.

She pulled her legs up onto the couch and took a deep breath. This of course was what she ached to hear, that her bad luck didn't matter. He—Chaos—was like an antidote, a glimmer of something, a refutation, however small, of Cooley's seamless, terrible version of the world.

"Melinda," she said. "She's . . ."

"Just traveling with me. She left her parents."

"No, I mean her *fur*."

Now he was the one who looked embarrassed. "There was a war," he said quietly. "It changed a lot of things, in Wyoming."

"A war?"

"Everyone remembers some kind of disaster. But it's different in different places."

"Why?"

He shook his head. "I don't know. People."

"People?"

"They make it different. Like the ones on the television . . ."

"President Kentman, and the government."

"Yes."

"I hate them." She huddled closer to him, thinking of war. Could it be worse in other places? Less like before? Maybe she was actually lucky. "But you"—now she held his hand—"you're running away. You *got* away."

He laughed softly. "I got here, you mean."

"Why are you laughing?"

"I'm not."

"Maybe you should stay here." Was it wrong to like him—*Chaos*, she reminded herself, though she still hadn't said the name aloud—because he represented something to her? He had nice eyes.

"Chaos," she said, trying it out. Then again: "Chaos?"

He answered her question by covering her mouth with his.

"Well," she said.

He kissed her again. She gently moved the empty soup bowl from his lap, onto the floor.

"It's been a long—"

"What, like beer?" she said, amused, but testing him.

"I didn't mean—I'm clumsy."

"Okay."

"Yes." He laughed again, which she liked now. "Okay."

"Unless you're tired—"

"No."

They kissed, and soon he pushed her shirt and bra up into a bunch under her arm on one side, exposing her breast to the cool air. She hid it by moving closer to him, and by tugging up his shirt and finding his chest to push against. He handled her a little fiercely, as if he was astonished.

That night, sleeping in his arms, she dreamed of him. *So soon,* she thought when she woke. It was a jealous dream. He was living in a house in the woods with a woman. Really living in the house, not just staying there for a few days. The house was his; she felt it in the way he moved through the rooms, the way he touched the objects in the house; they were his *belongings.* Odd, too, because of the way he'd left his car on the highway and wandered into her house and opened her fridge; he hadn't seemed like someone who understood what it was to own things. But this house was his. She was as jealous of that as the other thing, his being with the unfamiliar and beautiful woman. She was jealous, too, of the isolation, the way the house was alone in the woods. No children there. Just trees and water. When she considered the dream the next morning, she felt deeply ashamed.

There wasn't really enough room for Chaos beside Edie on the couch, and at dawn he crept upstairs to sleep on the double bed beside Melinda. But he woke alone, to sounds from the kitchen. He went downstairs and found them— Edie and Ray and Dave and Melinda—eating breakfast without him. Edie quickly got up, ladled out another bowl of oatmeal, and put it in front of an empty chair at the table. Chaos sat down. Edie smiled at him, nervously, and Melinda glared.

After breakfast Ray and Dave invited Melinda outside. Edie stood at the sink, washing dishes.

"There isn't enough in the house to eat," she said fretfully, her back to him. "Now, I mean, with you and Melinda—"

She dropped a plate, which shattered on the tile floor, and began hurriedly searching for a broom, but couldn't seem to find one. "People leave houses in the worst shape . . ."

He saw that she was waiting for some sign from him. So he went to her, and gently placed his hand on the small of her back. It was the only thing that didn't feel presumptuous or unnatural. She was stilled by the touch, the broken plate at their feet now irrelevant.

"Last night was good for me," she said, surprising him with the directness.

"Me too," he said.

"I forgot about this place, about Ian and all his luck nonsense."

"Good." He wasn't sure he should say that it was good for him for the opposite reason, because it made him remember. Chaos couldn't actually recall having sex with a real woman before. Even his fantasies had been pretty vague, until the series of dreams about Gwen. Now there was suddenly this.

He wasn't getting Edie and Gwen mixed up, he told himself. But maybe the dreams about Gwen had helped him to want Edie, to recall what it was to be with a woman. He was afraid of analyzing it further. Edie might see that he was confused and draw away.

He didn't want that.

They all piled into her car and rode into town, to the Vacaville Mall. The cars here were the old kind, that ran on gas, like back in Wyoming. The buildings here, too, suggested an intact version of the ruined townscapes back in Little America and Hatfork. Chaos didn't know what this meant. He kept feeling that somehow, intending to travel across land, he'd traveled through time instead.

The mall featured two distinct populations. The adults, who milled nervously, in couples or alone, greeting one another in clipped exchanges or not at all. And the kids, who ran and laughed and talked together, apparently in another world. Ray and Dave seemed to know anyone roughly their size. Melinda scampered after them, shadowing their conversations, sticking out her tongue when introduced, sticking out her tongue if challenged about her fur. Edie tried to keep them close at first, then compromised by making Ray agree to bring them all back to the car later. That decided, the three children disappeared.

"See these stores?" asked Edie once they were alone. She pointed out a drugstore, a magazine stand, a barbershop, and a hardware store. "I've worked in them all."

She seemed pleased to have this to point out to him. He didn't ask why she'd worked at so many places, or what her job was now.

"I don't know if I've ever worked in a store," he said instead.

"That must be strange," she murmured.

Chaos followed her into the supermarket, and pushed the cart as she gathered up a mound of supplies. None of the products had familiar names. Chaos picked up a box of cereal and showed it to Edie.

"Who's that?" he said, pointing. It was a face he vaguely recognized.

"Sandra Turfington, remember? She was on television last night."

"She makes cereal?"

"All the brands are endorsed by government stars."

A tune was playing, something arranged for strings, that he thought he remembered.

He asked Edie, and her odd, dismissive reply was "Muzak."

They took the groceries out to her car and loaded them into the trunk. The parking lot was full of kids, but not Ray and Dave and Melinda.

"There's no hurry," Chaos suggested.

"I know where they'll be," said Edie. "We might as well go round them up."

He followed. It was absurdly easy to tag along with her, to forget that they hadn't been doing this for years. It was almost a version of the Kellogg effect, he thought. Almost but not quite.

The kids were sitting together paging through comic books at a shallow storefront full of candy and magazines. The cover stories were all about the television and the government, even when they were versions of magazines like *Time* and *Rolling Stone* and *Playboy*, which Chaos knew from before. Nothing referred to anything outside Vacaville. Ray tugged on his mother's sleeve and pointed at what Dave was reading: a violent cartoon adventure starring Ian Cooley.

"I told you not to give him that," she said. "You should know better, Ray. You're the older one." She plucked the magazine away from Dave.

"Can I see that for a minute?" said Chaos.

Edie shot him a look.

"Never mind."

They drove home. Melinda sat in the backseat with Ray and Dave, pontificating, suddenly in her element. She told them about Hatfork and her former life in the desert; she explained how the television shows they liked were stupid because they weren't real; she told them how things would be different "when they grew up."

The boys had relaxed her, Chaos saw. With them she could stop trying to prove she was an adult. Yet for all her expansiveness she still seemed resentful towards him. She hadn't spoken to him directly, hadn't met his eye, since the night before.

After they unloaded the groceries and packed them into the kitchen, Edie went upstairs and the boys switched on the television. Chaos got Melinda alone for a minute.

"What's the matter?" he said. "You don't like me being with her?"

"I don't mind that," she said, her expression sardonic. "It's just you keep on dreamin' about that other one. That's what I don't like."

This said, she turned and skipped into the living room and joined the boys at the television.

Chaos still found it hard to believe he was projecting the dreams. Was he really like Kellogg? Would he go on helplessly broadcasting his dreams wherever he went?

Here in Vacaville he had managed to hold onto his previous identity, his memories of Hatfork and the trip west. He felt a certain pride in that. He wanted to believe he was growing stronger, building up an immunity to local effects, and Vacaville obviously had its share of changes. Chaos didn't remember much, but he knew people shouldn't have to move twice a week and work a different job every day. Or have their luck tested.

On the other hand, the effect was milder here. The Vacaville equivalents to Kellogg and Elaine—the government stars—lived in the media instead of invading dreams. And you could always turn the television off. So maybe his ability to hold onto his old self was just a part of local conditions.

Edie came back downstairs. "You want to meet Gerald?" she asked.

"Well, sure . . ."

"I have to drop the boys off," she said. "For the weekend. You don't have to come."

"No, I'd like to. It's just . . ."

"What?"

"Melinda will miss them."

She smiled but didn't say anything.

"Gerald lives in the Eastman-Merrill building," explained Edie during the drive. "He used to work there, before. When we separated, he had a kind of breakdown and went and hid there. He thought he could go back to the way it was before, or something. Cooley helped get him special permission to live there all the time. Otherwise Gerald would have had to go to a bad luck camp."

"What was it Cooley was saying about an elevator?" Chaos asked.

"Well, of course Gerald still feels the urge to move every Wednesday and Saturday. But he's afraid to leave the Eastman-Merrill building. So he keeps his bed and clothes and stuff in the elevator—"

"On Moving Day he changes floors," said Ray from the backseat.

Edie nodded, looking glum.

"It's fun," added Dave hopefully.

The Eastman-Merrill building was an abandoned office block in the middle of Vacaville's old downtown section. The neighborhood consisted of boarded-up storefronts, everything the mall had put out of business. Compared to the residential areas it was a ghost town. Edie had the key to a side door, and she led them inside, through the big empty lobby to the elevator. Ray ran forward and pressed the button marked UP.

The elevator doors opened to reveal a thin, pale man, Edie's age but with graying hair, sitting upright in a bed in the elevator, reading. He wore pajamas and heavy black wingtip shoes, and he had an array of pencils and toothbrushes sticking out of the pocket of his pajama shirt. The elevator was filled with ramshackle shelving, and the shelves were loaded with clothes, books, and empty bottles and cans.

"Gerald, this is Chaos and Melinda. Friends of mine."

"Hello," said Gerald amiably. "Do I remember you?"

"They're visiting," said Edie.

"Oh." Gerald smiled mildly. "From?"

Chaos opened his mouth to speak, but Edie quickly said, "Back east."

"Well. Nice, nice. I'd offer you a drink—"

The boys were already scrambling up onto their father's bed. The space that remained for standing was hopelessly narrow.

"We're not staying long," said Edie. The bag of groceries she'd brought she put onto the end of the bed. The elevator door started to close, but she nudged it back by pressing the safety bar.

"I saw Mr. Cooley," said Gerald. "He came to see how I was doing. We talked about the boys."

"Yes?" said Edie impatiently.

"He's very worried about you, Edie. He says that you're in trouble with your luck . . ."

"He's my trouble," said Edie.

"I think he cares for you," said Gerald. "He's certainly interested in the boys."

"I know," said Edie. "Listen, Gerald, I'll see you on Sunday. Have a good time."

"Yes, of course." Gerald's eyes seemed to mist over. "Edie, are you going to marry Mr. Cooley?"

"No, Gerald."

"I'm not saying I would object," said Gerald quickly. "I wouldn't want you to think that."

"No, Gerald. But I wouldn't anyway. Goodbye."

"He's a very important man," said Gerald. "He's done quite a bit for you, hasn't he?"

"That doesn't matter. Goodbye, Gerald."

"Edie—"

"Yes?"

"I haven't gotten any mail?"

"No."

From the way she said it Chaos suspected there hadn't been any mail delivered in Vacaville for a long time.

"Of course," said Gerald vaguely. "Well . . ." He waved his hand. The boys waved too. Edie let the elevator door close.

"God, he makes me angry," she said the minute they were back out on the street. She clattered ahead of them, towards the car.

"He's weird," said Melinda sympathetically. "That's all." She ran up and took Edie's hand, as though to fill the gap left by the boys. "There's a lot of weird people."

Chaos lagged behind. He got into the passenger seat without saying anything. Gerald and his elevator had made him think, for the first time since coming to Vacaville, of his candlelit projection booth back in Hatfork. His little world. Also, he was jealous of Cooley. He didn't understand what there was between Edie and the government man, but he knew enough to feel jealous. They drove back to the house in silence.

That evening nothing went right. Melinda was bored without the boys. When she switched on the television, Chaos tried to watch, but it wasn't the same without Ray's running commentary, Dave's wide-eyed engagement. Edie and he sat side by side on the couch, but he felt a million miles away, separated from her by the muddle of his jealousy and his shame about the dream of Gwen. Edie seemed tense, as though worrying over where Chaos would be sleeping tonight.

Chaos wanted time with her alone.

What he got instead was an unexpected visit from Cooley.

"I'm goin' upstairs," said Melinda, the minute Cooley walked into the living room.

"Can't you give me a break?" asked Edie.

"How's this for a break?" said Cooley, taking off his jacket and laying it across the back of the couch, their couch. "I came here to talk to Chaos."

"Well, I don't feel like seeing you tonight," she said. "You weren't invited."

"Come on, Edie." His voice was soft. "You know I don't need an invitation. Why make me say it?"

"You're the one who likes to pretend you're my *friend*," said Edie bitterly.

Cooley looked pained or compromised, but only for a moment. He turned to Chaos. "It's my job to keep track of Edie's progress, whether she wants to admit it or not." He sighed. "And that makes it my responsibility to try and help you understand what you're getting into here."

"Getting *into*—" Edie began.

"Shacking up with Edie here," said Cooley, ignoring her. "I don't know where you come from, but you aren't anybody's cousin. If you want to get set up in Vacaville, we can talk about that. But you're picking one ass-backwards way of getting started."

"He's going to tell you that bad luck is catching," said Edie in a rush, as though she could take Cooley's point away from him by stating it first. "He'll try to scare you. Everything he says is calculated to convince you you're in mortal danger just by being in the same house with me. It's meant to divide us."

"Edie," said Cooley warningly.

"I need a drink," Edie announced. "Anyone else?"

"I'll have a beer," said Cooley, his cops-and-robbers manner absurdly vanished. Chaos could see that all the man wanted was to be welcome in this house.

"A beer," echoed Chaos. "Sure."

"Let's sit down," said Cooley. He sat on the couch. Edie went into the kitchen. "I don't know how much you know about Edie's situation, Chaos, but it's not good. She scored in the lowest percentile—which is to say, really, that our tests don't even apply. We can't say just *how* bad your friend's luck actually is, only that eighty-five percent of the folks who score as low as she did end up in one of our resettlement centers. Not because we force them to go, which is what she's going to tell you in a minute. But because they run out of options."

Edie came in and handed them beer, in glasses. Before, she'd given it to Chaos in the bottle. Was she trying to impress Cooley? A bad sign.

Cooley sipped his beer, then went on. "What's more, the mess they make on their way down costs this county millions each year in damages, lost wages, that sort of thing. Which is why we have to track them."

"You drive people into the camps," said Edie fiercely, "and then you call it a statistic." She turned to Chaos. "Look what he's doing. Ever since I took the test, he's been hounding me. And he admits himself that they don't even know what the results mean!"

"It's a scientific test," said Cooley, smiling. "It tells us what we need to know about your probable future."

"You're making up my future as you go along," she said. "It's a self-fulfilling prophecy. You talk about luck, but you're the worst thing that's happened to me."

"You know that's not true, Edie."

"He wants me to feel sorry for Gerald," said Edie. "Gerald's craziness is supposed to be the fault of *my* bad luck."

"Edie's got the worst strain of bad luck," Cooley explained. "Fortunately it's fairly rare. She exposes the latency in the people around her, while maintaining a reasonable level of function for herself. She's always at the eye of the storm."

"Unfortunately," said Edie sarcastically, "I haven't been able to bring down any bad luck on Ian here. Yet."

Chaos sipped his beer and considered. There was a familiarity between them, as though their struggle was nothing more than a game. Flirting. Or was he failing to take it seriously enough? This is their world, he reminded himself.

"Okay," said Cooley. "Let's forget about Edie's luck for the moment. Let's talk about yours."

"Mine?" said Chaos.

"Yeah. Have you thought about coming in for the test? Sooner the better."

"I don't have luck," said Chaos. "Good or bad. I just go where I go, do what I do. No luck involved."

Cooley laughed. "Charming. Except science now tells us that luck is there whether you acknowledge it or not. And I'm afraid in your case I see the signs of a history of bad luck. Not even a latency so much as a full-blown case going completely ignored for lack of context."

No, thought Chaos. I'm not surrendering to the local crap this easy.

Cooley went on. "I wonder whether you can afford to aggravate it the way you are by cozying up with Edie here."

"Excuse me," said Edie, standing. "I think I'm going to be sick."

"What do you know about my history?" said Chaos.

"Well, let's see." Cooley's smile was enormous. "First of all there's that car you left on the highway. Cool car, incidentally; where'd you come by it? Too bad about the way it stopped working, though. Bit of bad luck there, I'd say, losing a car like that, a scientific wonder. Then there's that poor girl of yours; that's quite a disfiguring condition, though I'd say she's bearing up pretty well under the circumstances. And then there's your name. Chaos. That's not your real name, is it?"

"I guess not."

"But you can't remember your real name, can you?"

"No."

"Can't remember your name—that's bad luck in my book. But there's a lot you can't remember, all that stuff in the dream. The woman you're worrying about."

Chaos winced. Were the dreams leaking out that far? He avoided meeting Edie's eyes.

"Should I go on?" said Cooley. "My guess is you come from a place so fucked up that you think all your problems are normal. There are places like that out there."

Chaos didn't say anything.

"I think I've made my point. Of course, one of your worst patches of luck in a long time, though you don't know it yet, is running into old Edie here. That's as bad as luck can be. You've got nothing to offer each other but trouble."

"Puke, puke, puke," said Edie. She turned and went into the kitchen.

"I'm not saying you can't make it around here. Come take the test. I have a feeling you'll do all right, well enough to get by, anyway. I sense that about you. It's just the combination that's deadly."

You want Edie, Chaos was tempted to say. If that's bad luck, it's yours as well as mine.

Instead he said, "I don't believe in luck."

"No?" Cooley got up and put on his jacket. He adopted a pained expression. "She tell you about Dave?"

"What?" Chaos was confused. "What about him?"

"Ask her."

"What—"

"We'll talk more later. Take care." Cooley hurried out. Chaos heard his car start, then roar into the night. When the sound died away, the house was very quiet.

He found Edie sitting at the kitchen table with her arms crossed and her head rolled back, staring at the ceiling. "There's something I ought to tell you," she said after a while. "It might help you make up your mind about Ian."

"Go ahead."

"He's been coming on to me during this whole thing. He says that if I were with him . . . that things wouldn't be so bad for me."

"I could tell," said Chaos.

"He's so confident about his own luck. He says that what he's got in the luck department will more than make up for anything I lack. Those are his exact words. He says

107

that every time he takes the test, he scores better and better."

"But you haven't taken him up on it."

"I hate him."

Chaos could see that it was more complicated than that. She wanted to hate Cooley, but couldn't completely. It reminded Chaos of himself and Kellogg.

You have nothing to offer each other but trouble, Cooley had said. And it was probably true, but not because of luck. Chaos couldn't afford to stay here and let the local syndromes take root.

But then how could he help her in her struggle with luck? What could he offer a woman whose worst problem he couldn't even take seriously?

As for him, he wasn't even sure he had problems, not in that sense. His life was too full of gaps for that. The *world* had problems; he was just on the receiving end.

Or maybe Gwen was his problem. She was there, whatever boundary he crossed. But Gwen was hardly something Edie would want to help him with.

"He told me to ask you about Dave," Chaos said.

"He would do that," she said quietly.

"What did he mean?"

She sighed. "Dave's sick."

"Sick?"

"His kidneys. He was born defective. About a year ago they failed. His father gave him one; it had to be a close relative, me or Ray or Gerald. Now Dave and Gerald each have only one. There's nothing mysterious about it, though. It's just something that happened."

Chaos went over and put his hand on the nape of her neck.

"He wants you to think something bad will happen to

you if you stay with me," she said. "Like Gerald or Dave."

"He's jealous."

She nodded. "I don't care. He can keep bothering me if he wants. I don't even notice anymore. As long as he doesn't send me to a bad luck camp. It's awful. Everybody walking around on eggshells, wondering who's going to suddenly stub their toe or choke on a sandwich. I'd kill myself."

"That won't happen," said Chaos. "You won't go." He wondered what he meant by it.

They'd fallen asleep on the couch together, figuring out a way to sleep entwined so the narrow cushions were enough. But he was woken at dawn by the sound of an engine outside the house. The room glowed with yellow light. He lifted his head and listened for a minute as the sound peaked then faded. He closed his eyes again and pressed his face back against her hair. He heard footsteps on the porch. Someone knocked lightly on the door.

He got up and slipped into his clothes, thinking: Is this her bad luck or mine?

He opened the door and smelled cigarette smoke. The sun was just rising over the factory on the other side of the street, and the low hills behind the factory were covered with mist. Sitting on the edge of the porch was a man in a worn leather jacket holding a bright red motorcycle helmet, his back to the door. The man tossed a cigarette butt into the dewy patch of grass between the porch and the street and turned his head. "Hey, Everett," he said. "I wake you up?"

"Billy," said Chaos. The man's whole name was there in his memory: Billy Fault.

Fault grinned, got to his feet, stuck out his hand. Chaos stared at him. Eyes too close together, forehead too narrow, smile all gum. You would have to have reasons for being friends with a face like that; the face itself didn't supply any. Chaos suspected he'd had reasons sometime in the past. Seeing the face again was like finding the same odd-looking rock on a beach twice.

"Actually, I knew you were asleep. That's the only way I could find you here. Your dreams, I mean."

"Dreams?" Chaos didn't want to hear this.

"Yeah. I've been picking them up for a couple of nights now, finally tracked you down . . ."

"Tracked me down how?"

"Just tuning in on the dreams, Everett. Like tuning in on a radio station. I'm good at that, extra sensitive. Still took me all night, though."

"Where did you come from?"

"San Francisco, same as ever."

"As ever when?"

"We're all still there, Everett. Everybody except you. You're out here in Fuckaduck—excuse me, Vacaville."

Everybody except you. Who did that mean?

Gwen?

"—can't get over this place," continued Fault. "All these old cars, it's like some kind of old suburban nightmare Twilight Zone episode. Neeny-neeny, neeny-neeny . . ." He wiggled his fingers in front of Chaos's face. "You been here a long time?"

"No," said Chaos. "How far is it from here? San Francisco, I mean."

"It's about an hour's drive," said Fault. "Whole different world, though. You'll see. You're coming, right?"

"I don't know."

"Cale's expecting you." He stopped and studied Chaos's expression. "You remember Cale, Everett?"

Cale Hotchkiss. That name was there, too. "Yes," Chaos said.

"Good," said Fault, grinning. "Well, you and Cale have some catching up to do. Listen, you want to go for a ride with me? There's a guy out here I want to visit."

"All right," said Chaos.

At that moment Edie stepped out onto the porch, dressed in a robe and blinking in the new light.

"Edie," said Chaos nervously. "This is Billy. An old friend from, uh, San Francisco."

"Hello," said Edie, staring.

"Hi," said Fault.

"We'll be out for a while, I guess," said Chaos. "Go back to sleep if you want. I'll be back."

Now she looked at Chaos, her eyes questioning. But all she said was, "Okay. See you then."

"Good, okay," said Chaos. Fault lit another cigarette and started down the steps.

"Remember, I move today," said Edie.

"I'll be back before noon," said Chaos. He followed

Fault to the motorcycle and climbed onto the back of the seat.

"I try to visit this guy whenever I'm out this way," said Fault as they roared down the highway around the edge of town. "Each time I think it's probably the last time I'll see him. He's a survivor, though. Back in the sixties, they tried to give him the chair."

"The chair?"

"He was famous before. Part of some murder thing. He didn't do it, though. They used to say his girlfriend killed the President. He's just a classic scapegoat, told people things they didn't want to hear. There's never any percentage in being ahead of your time."

"Before?" It was all Chaos could do to get the question out. The wind was driving thin streams of tears out of the corners of his eyes.

"You know," said Fault. "Before all the rules changed."

Fault sped past the few cars on the highway and exited on the far side of town, onto a street filled with abandoned fast-food restaurants. He slowed down under a billboard that read: FOOZ! GET LOST IN THE WORLD'S LARGEST OUTDOOR MAZE! He stopped, cut the motor, and kicked out the stand. "That's where he lives."

"In the maze?"

"Yeah. He's the only guy around here who doesn't have to move all the time."

"I met someone who lives in an elevator," said Chaos.

Fault raised his eyebrows. "Vacaville used to be famous for two things: a mental hospital and a maze. Lucky's lived in both of them."

"I never heard of a place with a maze before."

"They modeled it on a famous maze in Japan, it was Japan's biggest tourist attraction. People coming from all over to get lost in this giant maze. But it didn't work in translation. I guess they needed a maze in Japan, where everything's neat and tidy. In America everybody's already wandering around lost. Even before the changes."

America. Chaos remembered that name, too. It was the name for everything, all of this: Wyoming, California, Utah, and lots more. It wasn't just the second word in Little America. There was a Big America, only it was so big, they didn't have to call it that.

"When the change came, Lucky and some other guys broke out of the hospital and hid in the maze. The others left, but Lucky never figured it out. He thinks he's still famous. The truth is nobody would even notice him now. I gave up trying to explain it to him."

Fault led him through a brightly painted carnival entrance and into the first chamber of the maze. The high walls were covered with graffiti, some arcane, some obscene. Fault followed a series of red spray-painted arrows, and Chaos, trailing after, quickly lost his bearings.

"Lucky," called Fault.

Chaos was full of questions, but he didn't know where to begin. He wanted to ask Fault about the changes. He wanted to ask about Gwen. It was Everett that Gwen loved in the dreams, so if Chaos was really Everett . . .

Chaos tried not to think about it.

They turned a corner and, in a roofed-over section of the maze, found Lucky. He lay on a plastic mattress in the shade, reading a coverless paperback and humming loudly. He looked up at them and smiled, displaying a mouthful of ruined gray teeth. His face was weatherbeaten and wrinkled, and surrounded by a fringe of ratty beard. His clothes were rags.

"Hey, Lucky," said Fault. He reached into his leather knapsack, pulled out a couple of cans of food, and handed them to the gaunt figure. Lucky sat up on his mattress and read the labels appreciatively, then tossed the cans onto a pile of junk under a rusted card table.

"You doing okay?" said Fault.

Lucky shrugged and smiled again. "Not *doing* anything."

"But you're hanging in there."

"Not hanging either," said Lucky, and tittered. "They tried hanging me, Jack, they did their best. No, I'm just sitting here in this maze trying to keep the rain out of my beard and the pigs off my tail. Who's your friend, Jack?"

"His name is Everett, Lucky."

"Everett. Hmmm." Lucky scratched at his beard, first thoughtfully and then like he'd found a flea. He seemed about to speak, but the moment stretched on and on.

"Lucky . . ." started Fault.

The old man suddenly straightened and glared at Chaos. "Why'd you come here?" he said.

"What?" said Chaos.

"Why'd you come here, *Everett?* What the hell are you doing in Vacaville?"

"Everett's been kind of out of things for a while," said Fault. "He's coming back to the city to see his old friends, get back in touch . . ."

"Why can't you let the man speak for himself, Jack?" Lucky waved his hand impatiently. "Get in touch, yeah, yeah. Where you coming from, Everett?"

"I was living in the desert," said Chaos.

"Oh? I used to live in the desert." He turned to Fault.

"That's not out of things, Jack. The desert is where it's at."

"I didn't mean anything," said Fault.

"Yeah, I know, that's the problem. You didn't *mean* anything." He turned back to Chaos. "Don't let this jerkoff put you down. It's hard coming in out of the desert. I ought to know, man. When you get back to the city, they don't understand you anymore. Not after you been in the desert."

"But Everett's from the city," said Fault. "He's coming back to his friends."

"This isn't about *friends*," said Lucky. "Is it?"

"I don't know," said Chaos.

"It's about a woman, isn't it? You're looking for a woman. That's what this is *about*. That's why Everett's coming back to the city. Am I right?"

"I don't know," said Chaos.

"Listen, Lucky," said Fault. "We've got to go."

"Yeah," said Lucky. "You always gotta go. See you later, man." He was back in his book before they'd turned the corner.

"Sorry about that," said Fault on their way out of the maze. "He doesn't usually get so weird."

"It's okay," said Chaos, still full of questions. He almost wondered if he was still on the couch beside Edie, dreaming. The maze was strange enough, in fact, for a Kellogg dream. But when they walked back out to the motorcycle and he saw the hills above Vacaville, he knew he wasn't dreaming. Or rather, that his life and his dreams were finally coming together.

"Billy?" he said.

"Yeah?"

"When did it happen? The changes, I mean."

"A few years ago."

"What happened?"

Fault grinned, showing his gums again. "That's a big question, Everett. Basically a lot of the old connections between things fell away, which gave people a chance to make up new ones. But the new ones don't always stick. That's my version, anyway. People like Cale have got a lot of complicated ideas about it."

"But there was a disaster of some kind."

"I don't personally consider it exactly a disaster . . ."

"There's a lot I don't remember, Billy."

Fault looked impatient with the conversation. "I'm hungry," he said. "Want to go find something to eat?" He patted the end of the seat.

"Sure," said Chaos. He got onto the motorcycle. The sun was high now, not quite overhead. He wanted to get back to Edie and Melinda in time for the move, but he was hungry too. He also wanted to ride on the motorcycle again, wanted to feel the wind. In fact, he sort of wanted to ride Fault's motorcycle without Fault on it. He didn't suggest it.

At the mall they got in line for one of the cash machines. Fault was armed with a bootleg bank card. He'd steered them confidently into the middle of town, seeming comfortable here, but they were drawing a lot of stares from the people in cars, on the sidewalks, and in the parking lot of the mall. Chaos hadn't seen any other motorcycles in Vacaville yet and he felt conspicuous.

Fault coaxed money out of the machine and led Chaos to Palmer O'Brien's, a restaurant named after a character Chaos had seen on Edie's television, a sort of rockabilly singer turned maverick government man. Inside, over the counter, was a huge blowup poster of O'Brien with a guitar, and the menu, which Chaos and Fault found printed on the laminated placemats at their booth, featured Palmer's

Breakfast Scramble, Palmer's Club Sandwich, and The O'Brien Boiled Dinner, all the hero's favorites. And apparently he really ate there, or had once: the walls featured several framed glossies of O'Brien at various booths and visiting the grateful slobs in the kitchen.

The restaurant was full but very quiet, and Chaos felt the weight of attention on them as they sat down. Were they just unfamiliar faces in a local hangout, or was there something in Fault's manner that said he didn't belong? Chaos hadn't attracted so many stares at the mall two days before, but then he'd been in Edie's company. Whatever the reason, when the waitress came to take their order, it was as though the whole restaurant was listening to see what they would eat.

Chaos ordered a ham sandwich. Fault studied the menu, keeping the girl waiting, then giggled to himself. "I don't know," he said, looking up, "I don't see it here . . ."

"Yes?" said the waitress impatiently. She was young and had a natural pout.

"Could you bring me Palmer O'Brien's Head on a Platter?"

It got so quiet in the room that Chaos could hear people shifting in their seats as they turned to look at Fault. The waitress stood back on her heels and scowled.

"Just kidding," said Fault, still giggling. "I'll have what he had . . ."

But she was walking away, and it wasn't clear that she'd heard him. She certainly hadn't jotted anything down; her pencil was back behind her ear.

Fault sank into the booth and screwed up his face sarcastically. Very gradually the conversations around them resumed.

"Fucking sheep," said Fault quietly. "I wouldn't live in this place if you paid me. Everybody in love with their little tin god soap opera stars . . ."

His voice wasn't low enough. Conversation died as people stopped to listen.

Fault's response was to bleat like a sheep, quite loudly.

"Billy," said Chaos softly, "maybe we should go somewhere else to eat—"

"No way," said Fault. "I'm hungry."

Now they were the center of attention. When the waitress came back out with a plate, the whole restaurant watched to see if she would go to their table. When she put a single ham sandwich in front of Chaos, there was a roar of whispers.

Chaos tried to defuse things by pushing the plate to a spot midway between them; the sandwich was cut in half, after all. But Fault pushed it back. "Where's mine?" he said loudly.

The waitress swiveled away.

"Shit," said Fault. He turned around and made faces at the people behind him. Chaos chewed the corner off a triangle of sandwich hopelessly, his hunger draining away.

Fault made the bleating sound again, then ostentatiously emptied the pocket of his leather jacket onto the table. Out tumbled a hypodermic syringe and a stoppered glass vial. Fault plunged the needle into the vial, drew the contents up into the syringe, and began rolling up his sleeve.

A man across from them rustled in the pocket of his coat, took out a ticket book and pen, and began scribbling, like a parody of the waitress taking their order. Then, as though the ice only had to be broken, five or six other people flipped open identical books and began racing to fill out the ticket. Fault just stared. The first man and a fat woman with her chubby son in tow jumped up at the same time and held finished tickets out to Fault.

"I was first," said the woman quickly, edging in front of the man.

"No. I saw them first," said the man tensely.

"We *all* saw them," said the woman. "That doesn't count for anything. We all saw them the moment they walked in here." She thrust her ticket at Fault, who was slapping at his arm to raise a vein.

"You'd better take it," she said. "I can write you another one for resisting citation."

"Stuff it, lady." He injected himself.

"Stop that," said a man who'd fallen too far behind in writing his ticket and given up. "You can't do that in here."

"You'd better take the ticket and leave," advised the woman.

"I don't think it matters," said Fault. He put the needle back onto the table. "I'm not from around here, see? And where I'm from, people don't go around giving each other tickets."

"Give it to *him*," said a man at the booth behind Fault. He pointed at Chaos. "He lives here. And he brought him here. He should know better."

"Fair enough," said the fat woman cheerily. "You take it." She handed the ticket to Chaos, who took it and put it in his pocket. He wanted to go, but felt paralyzed.

At that moment the waitress reappeared with a grease-smeared cook, his hair in a net, who stood glowering behind her.

"Get out," she said.

"Fuck you," said Fault.

"I called the government," she said. "They're on their way. You'll be very sorry if you don't go. Now."

"I'm not leaving until I get my sandwich. Or until you make Palmer O'Brien come here himself."

"That can probably be arranged," growled the cook. "But you won't be laughing long, if it comes to that."

"In fact, I want Palmer O'Fucking Brien to bring me my sandwich and serenade me while I eat," jeered Fault. "That would do the trick."

"Okay, you jackass," said the cook, pushing past the waitress and grabbing Fault by the collar. He jerked him up out of the booth and pushed him towards the door. Chaos took Fault's motorcycle helmet, leaving the vial and needle on the table, and followed the cook and Fault out the front door of the restaurant. The man who'd written the first ticket, the waitress, and several others followed. Outside, a crowd from the mall was already gathering around Fault and the cook.

"Pay up," said the cook, shoving Fault backwards.

"I didn't get anything," said Fault. He spat on the ground between them and straightened his collar defiantly.

Several of the people around them were busily writing up tickets. "He won't take it," someone warned. Someone else said: "That one's staying with Gerald Bitter's ex-wife. If he won't take it, you can send it to her."

Chaos pushed forward past the cook and handed Fault his helmet. "Let's go," he said. Fault spat again, but the cook didn't notice; he was distracted by someone's trying to give *him* a ticket, for leaving his post in the restaurant. "—thinks he's on TV," said a woman disdainfully.

The event degenerated into squabbles between the Palmer O'Brien loyalists who'd been in the restaurant and others who'd only seen the cook roughing up Fault outside.

The crowd buzzed with the news that the government had been summoned: who would appear? Someone claimed she'd seen President Kentman himself. Chaos and Fault slipped away to the parking lot.

Fault, it turned out, didn't know the way back to Edie's house. He'd only gotten there the first time by following Chaos's dreams, he explained again. They found the house by taking the highway all the way out of town, to the east, then doubling back, until Chaos spotted the right overpass. His pink-splattered car was gone from where they had abandoned it—a loose end the government didn't permit, apparently. It made Chaos think of Melinda, their trip together. He felt a pang of guilt.

As Fault slowed in front of the house, Chaos could see that something wasn't right. Edie's car was gone, and another was parked in its place. There was a spotted black-and-white dog leashed to the front porch, and it barked at them as they dismounted.

"Shit," said Chaos.

"What?"

"Moving Day."

"Oh man, I'm sorry."

Chaos went up the porch steps, let the dog sniff his hand, and knocked on the door. The woman who answered was middle-aged and black. "Sorry to bother you," said Chaos. "The people who were here before . . ."

"Yes?"

"Did you see them?"

"They were a little late getting out, as a matter of fact. How can I help you?"

"Was there a little girl with, uh, fur all over her body?"

"Yes. Her and an older woman." The black woman

peered out past Chaos at Fault and his motorcycle. "But who's asking?"

"You don't know where they went, do you? They didn't leave any word?"

"No. I'm sorry." She shut the door.

As Chaos walked back down the porch steps, Cooley drove up and parked behind Fault's motorcycle, then got out and strolled over to where Fault was standing. Chaos hurried to intercept him.

"Hello, Chaos," said Cooley. "Looking for Edie?"

"Well actually—"

"I know. I just saw her. She's all worried, says you went off with some old friend. I told her to relax. Said I'd go back and find you. This your pal?"

"Yeah, Billy—"

"Ian. Pleased to meet you."

"Yeah." Fault shook his hand.

"Where you from?"

"San Francisco." Billy sounded nervous.

"Really. I haven't been to the city for a while. What brings you this way?"

Fault jerked his thumb, indicating Chaos. It should have looked casual, defiant, but Fault's expression made it come off as tongue-tied.

"Old pals, eh?" Cooley's tone was insinuating. "Heard you got into a little bit of a fuss up at the mall."

Fault took a step backwards. He seemed cowed. Chaos wondered if Fault was sensitized to Cooley's status as a government star, tuned into the ideology like everyone else around here. It didn't make sense otherwise: Cooley wasn't any more imposing than the cook at the mall, and he wasn't backed by a crowd.

"A bit of one," said Chaos, answering for Fault.

There was a moment of tense silence, then Cooley laughed, loudly. Fault stared, then tittered too, sycophantically. He suddenly reminded Chaos of Edge.

"Bit of one," Cooley repeated. "They give you a ticket?" He held out his hand.

Chaos dug it out of his pocket, and Cooley examined it. "Well, well." He tore it in half and then into quarters, and let the pieces flutter into the mud of the road. "Edie doesn't need any more of those at the moment. This one wasn't her fault, anyway. For once. Or your fault, for that matter. Except it was your bad luck that brought this little shithead into town."

"What?" said Fault.

"You heard me," said Cooley. "You used a fake card in that cash machine. Stole money from the folks that live here. We don't need that fancy San Francisco crap around here. Give me the card."

Fault handed Cooley the bootleg cash card, and Cooley pocketed it. "Okay, Motorboy. Basically I want you out of town. Except you can give your pal Chaos a lift to Edie's new place. So go sit over there on the porch while Chaos and I have a word or two."

Fault walked over to the porch without a murmur.

"You and Edie are a real magical combination, Chaos. Bad luck is exponential, you know. If you're going to add that much bad luck to your life, you better upgrade your radar and quick. Learn to spot trouble like this one a mile off." He jutted his chin at Fault.

"Where's Edie?" asked Chaos.

"I'll give you her new address, Chaos. But I want something in exchange. I want you to say you'll come in Monday morning and take the test."

"I could find Gerald's building," Chaos pointed out.

"Wait there until she comes to pick up the boys. I don't need your help."

"You don't understand. You think I'm jerking your chain. But I'm trying to help. I'm saying take the test, get squared away with us, get on the rolls. We'll sign you up for a work shift, too. I'm saying welcome aboard, stick around a while. The test is just the way we do things around here. Not everybody's all hounded and paranoid all the time, Chaos. Not everyone's like Edie. You'll find that out if you give it a chance."

"You want me away from Edie."

"Okay, Chaos." Cooley grinned his wide grin. "Whatever. Here I am about to give you her address, and trying to help you get lined up for a test, which if you're going to stick around here, with Edie or not, is a must, and you're suggesting you might prefer to spend the night with Gerald instead. Your choice."

Chaos didn't say anything.

"Edie's due for a work shift Monday. She can drop you off at my office on her way to punch in. Test takes about an hour and a half."

"I'll think about it." Saying this, he felt defeated.

"Good enough."

Cooley gave him directions, and Chaos immediately felt cheated; Edie had moved just a few blocks away. "And I don't mean to be harsh—" Cooley continued.

"Yes?"

"But after that sonofabitch takes you to her place, I want him gone."

They drove off, Chaos and Fault towards Edie's new apartment and Cooley in the opposite direction. Fault began muttering oaths the minute Cooley's car was out of sight; Chaos didn't ask him why he'd waited so long.

"I've got to get some sleep," Fault said absently when they pulled up in front of the three-story apartment building. Edie was at the top. "Otherwise I'd stick around."

"That's all right," said Chaos. He wanted to go upstairs. He needed to think.

"So you get things settled," continued Fault. "I'll be back to pick you up tomorrow, okay?"

"What?"

"Bright and early, while this town's still asleep, so we won't run into any of your fascist friends, you know? Just slip out while they're fixing their morning coffee."

"Well . . ."

"You're coming to the city, right? Cale's expecting you."

"I don't know. I don't know what I'm doing." He didn't want to leave Edie. But he didn't want to take the luck test, either. It couldn't hurt to have Fault come back, he decided. He wouldn't go if he didn't want to.

"Here," said Fault. He dug in his satchel and pulled out a black plastic cartridge. "Cale wanted me to give you this. You need a VCR to watch it."

"VCR?"

"Ask Edie. They're built into most of the televisions around here, I think. She'll know."

Chaos took the cartridge.

Fault lit a cigarette and struck a pose on his motorcycle, as though reconstituting his image as a rebel after Cooley's dismantling. He strapped on his helmet and revved the engine. "See you tomorrow, Everett."

Everett. Chaos had momentarily forgotten.

He took the name, and the cartridge, upstairs.

The tape was about three minutes long. The first two and a half were Cale—Cale Hotchkiss—talking at the camera, a tight headshot. The first thing he said was, "Listen, Everett: do you remember when we were twelve or thirteen, and we broke into the train yard?"

Chaos remembered. They'd walked the tracks to the end of the line, to the yard where the trains sat overnight, with spray cans for painting graffiti. They'd covered one car with paint from top to bottom, then gone uptown to wait for it to roll through the station, except they'd fallen asleep on the bench on the platform and missed it. Cale had been his best friend. The question was obviously meant to trigger the memory, and it had worked.

Clearly Chaos was going to have to get used to the name Everett.

"I want to see you," Cale went on. "I'm glad you're coming back. There's something I think you can help me with."

He paused, looked away from the camera, and Chaos felt that he ought to say something, answer. The face and voice on the tape were in some way more real than anyone or anything he'd encountered in a long time. Through them he could almost taste his life before the break.

"You were right, Everett," continued Cale. "All the stuff you used to say about what mattered, you were right. Everything else is just what you have to work through to get back to what you know matters when you're twelve or thirteen." Cale paused. "The change is weird. When you're young, you'd like to remake everything, you want the world to be growing up with you. Now it's sort of true."

Chaos wanted to believe that this dark-eyed man was his friend. He wanted it to be true that Cale needed him, missed him. Knew him. Chaos wanted to be known, known in a way that would help him know himself.

"We'll talk when you get here," said Cale. "I don't want to overwhelm you. I'm just worried that you might not remember enough to know to come back. That you'll get this close and then wander away again."

Cale looked away from the camera, and the screen went blank. Then there was another clip, this one very short. A woman stood against a black backdrop, wearing a black suit, so she was barely more than face and hands floating in a mist of static. She pushed her hair back, and the camera moved in closer. She was beautiful.

It was Gwen, and the neutral space she inhabited on the television screen was just like the darkened room where Chaos had met with her in his dreams.

"Everett." She blinked and looked down. "Cale says you're really there. He says he knows from his dreams—but I don't dream anymore." She looked up and laughed softly at whoever was behind the camera. "I don't know what to say. Uh, come and see me, okay, Ev? I'd like to see you. That's all, I guess."

The camera held her for a few seconds more, and then the screen went black.

Edie had shown Chaos how to use the VCR, then sat back in a chair and watched the tape in silence. But when Gwen appeared on the screen, she got up and went into the bedroom, closing the door behind her. Melinda just sat on the floor and fidgeted. When Chaos switched the television off, she made a sour face and said, "Where'd you get that?"

"A guy gave it to me," he said absently. "Guy I used to know."

"The motorcycle man?"

"Yes."

"What are you going to do?"

"I don't know." He got up and knocked on the bedroom door, and when Edie didn't answer, he went in. She was sitting on the edge of the bed beside a pile of clothes.

"Somebody left some old clothes here," she said. "They might fit you. You have to wash the ones you're wearing."

"I thought you couldn't take anything."

"Clothes are up for grabs. You're supposed to take them with you. So if they're left behind, you can have them."

"Okay," he said. "I'll try them on. Thanks."

She got up nervously. "When you change, put your old clothes in the bathroom. I'll wash them and hang them up."

"I think I'm going to San Francisco tomorrow."

"So?"

"They probably wouldn't dry in time."

"They smell," she said. "Either wash them or throw them out." She turned away from him and left the room. He followed her out, past Melinda, who'd switched the television back on, and into the kitchen.

Edie began to inventory and rearrange the items in the refrigerator and cabinets, but from her manner Chaos suspected she'd done this once already. Neither of them spoke. After a few minutes she pulled out a box of crackers and a hand-labeled plastic container of peanut butter and began jamming roughly smeared crackers into her mouth.

"What's the matter?" said Chaos.

"I don't like your new friends," she said thickly, through a mouthful of crackers.

"They're not my new friends, they're my old friends."

"Well, I don't like them, especially the one this morning, the only real one. Mr. Leather Jacket. He's awful, Chaos. And he's getting you in trouble already."

Chaos didn't want to argue Fault's merits. He wasn't sure Fault had any. "What do you mean, the only real one?"

"The other two are just pictures," she said. "On television. They're like your dreams. I don't believe they're real. They're from inside you."

"That doesn't make sense. It's a tape, Edie."

"Well, a lot of things don't make sense. I've learned not to trust what I see on television, that's all. People telling you they're your friends, looking all charismatic. I thought you knew better."

"This isn't television like you have here. It's a tape. It's images of people I know talking to me on a tape."

"Well, it sure looked like television to me."

"You're not being reasonable, Edie. Besides, that's not the point. That's not why I have to go. Ian says I have to take his test. He won't leave us alone, Edie. He'll do whatever it takes to split us apart."

Her eyes grew wide and hopeful. "That's not important, Chaos. We can deal with Ian—"

"He's from the government, he can do anything he wants. He's only holding back because he thinks he can have you. If I stay, he'll ruin your life and call it luck. He'll take you away from your kids."

She was quiet for a minute, and then said, half to herself, "You're only trying to make it seem like it's for me that you're going away."

"No . . ."

"Yes. You tell me it's for my own good. And then Ian will come and tell me it's more proof of my bad luck. You'll just make him right if you go. Everything happens to me. Ian's right."

"No. If I stay and take his test, then we'll both have to do what he says. I'm leaving because I don't believe in luck."

"Why can't you be honest? You're leaving because you want to see that woman."

The word *woman* sat there between them, ringing in the silence. Chaos couldn't think of anything to say to displace it.

"It's okay," said Edie. "You have to find out. You can't

just keep wondering. I understand. You have to go." She hesitated, and added, "I can't live with your dreams anymore anyway. I feel like I'm sleeping with *her*."

"It's not just about her," said Chaos. "It's about me. Who I was before."

"Okay." She ate another cracker. "I don't want to talk about it anymore."

He felt beaten, despite getting what he wanted.

"What about Melinda?" she asked.

"Can she stay here with you?" He didn't want Melinda along. And Edie might see it as a promise that he'd come back. He didn't know if it was.

She hesitated, then said, "All right."

But Melinda was standing in the kitchen doorway. The television played unwatched in the other room.

"You jerk," she said. "You're going to see that girl."

"I'll be gone a day or two," he said, fumbling.

"What, you think I want to go with you?" Her eyes were wet, but her scowl didn't allow any weakness. "You jerk. You're just like Kellogg with your stupid dreams. I hate it."

Melinda and Edie slept in the two bedrooms that night, and Chaos sat in the living room watching the television until he fell asleep with it on. He woke to sunlight, a test pattern, and the sound of Fault's motorcycle revving down in the street.

Everett remembered San Francisco.

Fault took him through it the long way, through the Submission District, before climbing the hill into No Alley. The streets of the Submission were alive, teeming, the solar neon glowing, the sidewalks hectic with peddlers, the roads clotted with traffic, animal, mechanical, and pedestrian. Steambath proprietors stood beside their cubicles hawking quarter-hour sessions to the street people. Customers squirmed into taquerias past drunks and children and pick-pockets and drunken pickpockets and child pickpockets and drunken children. Half-completed sex-changes leaned out of the windows above the shops and shrieked to one another across the street. The stream of traffic parted, scooting dogs, vendors, and Fault's motorcycle up onto the sidewalk to make way for a gigantic two-wheeled RVcycle, its bloated kitchenette body aloft with antigrav.

It was just as Everett remembered, but it was changed, too. Or maybe it was Everett who had changed. The city had always been in ruins, a place that had never cohered. There were probably people living here who thought that there had been no rift. Everett suspected that if he stayed in the city, he might eventually come to agree with them.

Fault tried to swing back into the street, but a corroded televangelist robot staggered into their path, blocking the motorcycle. Its ferroplastic limbs creaked with every movement, and when it knelt to bless the ground, Everett saw that strips of shredded rubber hung from its soles. Fault honked his horn. The televangelist looked up. The computer graphic face of its television head babbled and ranted quietly as its video eye stared, taking them in.

Everett remembered the machines, though he'd never before seen one in such disrepair. Ordinarily, they'd launch into street-corner sermons at every opportunity, trying to convert unbelievers to a variety of faiths. This one was preaching to no one but itself.

Fault honked again. The face on the screen, a corpulent, middle-aged country preacher, wrinkled its chin and frowned. "Lost sheep," it muttered. "In need perhaps of a shepherd?"

"Get out of the way," said Fault.

The televangelist only planted itself more firmly and lifted an accusing finger. "Or devils, perhaps . . ."

"Oh, Christ," said Fault, and he began backing up,

pushing with his heels on the pavement, to get clear of the robot.

"You speak the name of your master, devil," fumed the televangelist. Pamphlets spilled out of the pockets of its ragged tunic, littering the sidewalk.

Fault rolled clear and then sped away around the robot, back into the crowded street. Soon they were out of the Submission and into the hills.

Everett remembered Fault now. It was with as much contempt as affection. Everett and Cale had been friends, Fault a third who dogged their steps, the last to get any joke. That was how the memory went. Everett felt stupid that Fault had herded Chaos blindly around Vacaville, getting him into trouble at the mall. Everett could have avoided it easily, but Chaos hadn't known any better.

Stupid Chaos, Everett thought. But he got me through.

No Alley was shrouded in mist. As they rode into it, Everett thought suddenly of the green. He shook it off. A seamless green fog in the mountains was something quite different from the bank of white that covered the hills of the Alley. San Francisco was supposed to be foggy.

Still, they seemed to have ridden out of the city into a zone of erasures. An occasional rooftop broke through the cloud, and the street was visible at either side. But while the streets of the Submission had been full of parked or junked cars, here the curb was empty, and past it gates and stairways led up into the haze.

When Fault stopped at the gate of the Hotchkiss house, Everett felt a shock of recognition. The house loomed behind a veil of cypress trees, aloof and protected. The upper story was mostly glass, the Victorian architecture ripped out and replaced with a modern greenhouse window. It seemed to reflect glints of sunlight, though there was no sun, and

Everett's eyes hurt when he looked up at it. Fault parked the motorcycle just inside the gate, and they walked up the driveway to the house together in silence.

Fault went down the concrete steps to the basement apartment. Everett looked at the upstairs doorway, remembering more. "Cale still lives with his father?"

"You'll see."

The basement had been headquarters for Everett and Cale, the place where they'd told the jokes that Fault got last. Now it had reverted to some primal hideout. The floor was littered with laundry and bedclothes, and Cale's books and computers were gone.

"Where's Cale?" asked Everett.

"This is my place now," said Fault. "Want a beer?"

Everett shrugged.

"Here." Fault went to the refrigerator, a giant, battered, eggshell-colored antique patched with glue spots from scraped-away decals. Its door was padlocked. Fault dug in his pocket for a key and undid the lock. When he opened the door, Everett caught sight of the contents: six-packs were jammed in sideways to fill the lower shelves, and the top shelf and door racks were filled with stoppered test tubes.

Fault handed Everett a beer, took one for himself, and carefully repadlocked the door. Everett examined the bottle. The cap had been screwed back on with a tool, pliers maybe, that had sheared away the metal ridges as well as parts of the glass threading. The label, pasted on over the bleached remains of a previous one, read: WALT'S REGULAR ALE. He tasted it: homemade. A step above the bathtub gin he'd been drinking in Hatfork, but only a step.

"Where's Cale?" asked Everett again. He thought, too, Where's Gwen? but didn't say it.

"Relax," said Fault, pausing to chug at his beer. "You ought to see Ilford first."

"Ilford?" Everett was unsure of the name.

"Cale's dad. He's been waiting for you," said Fault, slurping. "He wants to see you, welcome you back."

"You told him I was coming here?"

"Didn't have to tell him. Your dreams get around, Everett." The nursing sounds accelerated until Fault had reduced his beer to a bottle of suds. He set it on the floor and said, "Let's go."

Everett followed him outside, up the flagstone steps to the front entrance of the main house. Fault left the door to the basement apartment ajar. With his beer and test tubes secure, there was nothing else in the apartment worth protecting, apparently. The fog had tucked in closer, now veiling even the gate where Fault had parked the motorcycle. At the door he turned and took the half-full beer from Everett's hand and hid it in the bushes at the side of the doorway. "Get that later," he said, as if it was an explanation.

They went into the house, and Everett felt his senses immediately overwhelmed. The living room was like a museum, the walls covered with paintings, the antique furniture polished to a creamy glow. The glass coffee table held an ornamented golden clock with a pendulum that clacked softly and sent a shivery golden reflection running back and forth across the glass. Everett was hypnotized by the room, so dazzled and drunk that he wanted to lie down. After the apartment downstairs, not to mention the homes in Vacaville, it was like stepping onto a movie set. Fault immediately seemed froglike and compromising; Everett wanted to step away from him, not be associated.

As strange as the room was, it carried the same charge as Cale Hotchkiss's face on the videotape: Everett *remembered* it. Then Ilford Hotchkiss stepped into the room, and Everett had to wonder if he really remembered anything at all.

He was too young to be the father of the man on the tape. He was exactly Everett's size, but so upright and hard, his hair and eyes each like glossy stone, like marble, that he seemed immense, a portion of the room that had broken off to offer a handshake. At the same time he was so groomed and fine that he seemed miniaturized, a jewel-like mechanism like the golden clock or one of the bonsai trees that lined the mantel. His hair was gray at the temples, but the gray seemed just a polite touch, a ruse. Like the room, he looked better than anyone Everett—or Chaos—had ever seen.

He also looked too much like his own son. A part of Everett was sure this *was* the one on the videotape, altered just enough to impersonate his own father, and he almost blurted "Cale—" as the man stepped up and took his hand.

"Billy," Ilford said, looking straight into Everett's eyes, "why don't you fix us a drink? Scotch all right, Everett?"

Everett nodded absently, and Fault scurried over to the bar. Ilford led Everett to a chair and seated himself on the couch on the other side of the glass table and shimmering clock. Fault handed them each a drink in a square, beveled glass, a sharp contrast to the recycled beer bottle Everett had just surrendered. The glass weighed so much, it felt magnetized to the floor, and the liquor smelled so rich and intense, it didn't seem to need drinking.

"It's extraordinary to see you, Everett." Ilford's smile was waxen, and his eyes bored into Everett's, searching—for what? Recognition? Complicity?

Everett took a sip of the whiskey, stared into the glass.

"I heard you've been in Vacaville," said Ilford evenly.

"Yes."

"Quite a scene."

"Yes."

"I mean, what did you think of it?"

"Like you say, quite a scene." Everett wanted to grab the man and scream, Who are you? Where's Cale? Where's Gwen?

"Well, compared to that scene I think we've got something pretty good here."

"You mean San Francisco?"

"More specifically the Alley. It's very local. I'm sure you've noticed how local things can get nowadays."

"You don't have . . ." Everett waved his hand, wanting it to be understood without his having to say it. "You don't have someone in charge here? You know, that way?"

Ilford laughed without opening his mouth, then said, "Not that way."

Fault came back with his own drink, a glass almost level to the top with brown liquor. "Everett doesn't need convincing," he said, grinning. "He came halfway across the fucking country to find us."

Everett took another gulp of his whiskey, then raised his eyes and considered again the man seated on the other side of the table. Ilford Hotchkiss appeared to waver in and out of focus, as though struggling unsuccessfully to cohere, but when his eyes met Everett's, he reassembled his tense smile, and the rest of him gelled around it. Am I drunk? Everett wondered. He set the tumbler down with a too-loud thwack on the glass and leaned back in his chair, shutting his eyes. He wanted to squeeze away the shimmer of the room, the overprecise details in the paintings and bonsai trees and Ilford's confusing face, but they remained etched into his vision, as though printed on the inside of his eyelids. And his ears couldn't shut out the racket of the clock.

"Something the matter?" said Ilford.

"He's beat," said Fault.

Fault and Ilford, the hovering pair of them, were absurd and horrible. They were gargoyles at the rim of a void, a void consisting of the absence of Cale and Gwen. Cale and Gwen were his true destination, the lure that brought him here and held him.

But he was stuck instead with Fault and Ilford.

What kind of deal had been struck in this house?

He was suddenly desperately weak. A straight line ran from Chaos's argument with Edie the night before to Everett's pouring whiskey on top of beer just now. It was too much, he was too many people, one too many at least. And so was Ilford Hotchkiss.

It was raining when he woke very early the next morning. The house was silent. He'd been put to bed in a spare, clean room whose windowpane was gently raked by wet eucalyptus leaves. He slipped out from under the covers, dressed in new clothes from the dresser, and tiptoed downstairs. The rain had failed to disperse the fog; the house was still isolated, like a figurine in a milky fishbowl. He went outside, still in his bare feet, and stood in the cold wet wind and breathed the morning air. The water spilled off the roof in a line of drops onto the flagstones that led around the corner of the house and down to the basement apartment. He tiptoed back through the house and upstairs to put on his shoes, then went through the rain down the steps.

There in the squalor of what had been Cale's apartment sat Fault, slumped in a chair by the window, watching the rain. He turned and smiled vaguely at Everett, and said, "Up early."

Everett felt voiceless, as though he'd wandered from his bed only in a dream.

Fault waved carelessly. "Sit down."

Everett sat in the free chair where it stood, rather than pulling it up closer to Fault.

"You can't tell Ilford," said Fault warningly.

"Tell Ilford what?"

"That Cale's here."

"That shouldn't be a problem, Billy. Because Cale's not here."

"Oh, he's here, all right."

"What do you mean?"

"I visit with Cale every morning when it rains. Lately it rains every morning."

Fault was insane, Everett saw now. But, then, where did the video come from?

"I mean, he's not here *now*." Fault jumped up from his seat, suddenly animated. "He wore off just before you came in. But there's more."

"More where?" Everett didn't mind playing along.

"In the fridge."

"There's more Cale in the fridge."

"Right. My stash."

Everett sighed. "Well, then, break some out. Don't be selfish."

"But you can't tell Ilford." Fault began digging in his pocket for the padlock key.

"I won't."

Fault opened the lock and leaned into the refrigerator. He emerged with one of the stoppered test tubes in one hand, a syringe in the other, and nudged the door shut again with his foot.

"Here you go," he said musingly, then uncorked the vial with his teeth. "Gib me an arb," he said around the cork as he deftly plunged the syringe so that it filled with the contents of the tube.

"What?"

Fault spat out the little cork and said: *"Arm."*

Everett stared dumbly.

"C'mon, roll up your sleeve."

The rain clattered on the stones outside, heavy and inevitable. Beyond that there was only fog. Everett could feel the weight of the house above them, the gleaming living room, the golden clock, the cabinet full of amber whiskey, all pressing down on the squalid apartment. Fault loomed towards him, smiling raggedly, the ready syringe held softly at his waist. Everett imagined that his entire journey from Hatfork had led to this moment, to this phantom house in what should have been a city but was only an island in fog, and that his destination had been condensed to a pinprick point. He rolled up his sleeve and held out his arm.

"Everett."

Cale was sitting across from him, on an invisible chair in a featureless expanse of blank space. It was the Cale from before, the Cale from the videotape he had viewed as Chaos back in Vacaville. The friend he remembered. But, actually, couldn't remember, not in any way that held together or matched what he'd found here.

Fault, the room, the window, were all gone.

"You're here," said Cale. He smiled, leaned forward, but didn't extend his hand.

"I guess I am," Everett heard himself say.

Anyway I'm *somewhere*, he thought. And you're in it, this somewhere I'm at. We're in it together.

"There's a lot we have to talk about."

There was a staggering understatement. "Your father—" Everett began.

"Fuck Ilford. He's not important. Leave him out of this."

"Okay," said Everett.

It made a kind of symmetry, at least, with Fault's injunction against telling Ilford about Cale.

Everett turned his head, wanting to grasp the nature of this null-zone that had replaced the world. Behind him lay only depthless gloom, a gray that might be as near as his eyelids, as far as the stars. Staring at it produced a sensation at once vertiginous and claustrophobic.

He turned back. Cale was seated at a comfortable distance. He was the only point of reference, the only marker of scale.

"Cale—"

"Yes?"

"There's a lot I don't remember. Or understand."

"You remember me?"

You as a drug in a test tube, or as a ghost lurking behind your father's features? Everett wanted to ask.

No, the one he should remember was a man living in a basement apartment, a friend.

With all he'd reclaimed when he rode on Fault's motorcycle out of Vacaville and into San Francisco, Everett was still adrift. And here, in a city of erasures, things had narrowed to him and Cale.

Ask me the question again about the train yard, he thought, wanting to relive the tangibility of that moment.

"I remember you from before," he said simply.

"And then what?"

"And then I remember Hatfork. A town in Wyoming. Being a man named Chaos."

"You don't remember the break?"

"No."

"Don't worry about it. It's like a jump cut in a movie. Everyone is missing something."

Like you, for instance, Everett wanted to say. Missing a body.

Then he wondered: Was that better or worse than what he was missing?

"I came to see Gwen," Everett said. "I remembered her. That's what brought me back."

"I know."

"She was on the tape that Fault—"

"You can see her in a minute."

Cale said this casually, but it wasn't a casual thing to Everett. The idea that Gwen could be a minute away, whatever kind of minute that might be, was disturbing.

"First tell me about Hatfork," Cale went on. "I know some of it from your dreams, and from Fault. But I want to hear it from you. Tell me about Kellogg."

So Everett laid it all out. Kellogg and Little America, the cars, the hoards of cans, then Melinda, the trip west, and Edie. He was amazed at the flow of words, the sound of his own voice; it was the most he'd said aloud for as long as he could remember. He realized, reaching the end, that he was trying to strike a bargain, one where he'd get back as much as he gave.

Afterwards, however, they sat in silence. Cale looked preoccupied, staring off into the blankness of the space they shared, as though he saw something there.

"It doesn't matter," said Cale finally. "I should get you to Gwen before the dose wears off."

"I told you what I know," said Everett.

"I'm sure you did," said Cale. He seemed dissipated. "It's funny, though. You have a way of leaving yourself out of the story." He reached into the void at his left and turned an invisible door handle, which clicked audibly.

"What do you mean?" said Everett, watching as a doorway swung open. Beyond it lay a greater darkness. He craned his neck, tried to focus, but couldn't see anything. Staring only made the gloom dance with illusory swirls of static.

"You deserve more credit, that's all." Cale's voice had grown dim. "You had a lot to do with the things you saw." He pointed. "Go inside."

Without intending to move, Everett fell forward and through the doorway.

The white outlines of a room were sketched into the black space. He turned back, to see Cale still seated in his nothingness. "Go," Cale croaked.

Everett turned and swam forward.

She sat on the edge of a white-outlined bed. She was dressed in something black that merged with the background, so that her face and hands were radiant, afloat. It was the image from the tape, and from his dreams. Gwen.

"Everett." She moved the hair from her face and smiled shyly. "I've been waiting . . ." She looked down, her hair falling again. When she looked up a moment later, her eyes were shiny with tears. "Is it really you?"

"Yes," he blurted.

"Cale said you were coming. From the dreams. I couldn't believe it. Even Fault, everybody dreaming about you. Except me."

"I can't control it, the dreaming—"

"I know. It doesn't matter." She looked into his eyes, then away. "Come here."

He went and sat beside her on the bed. He felt her weight as her hip slid against his. He touched her shoulder. She reached up and took his hand, brought it to her lap. Their fingers curled together.

"I haven't been the same without you," she said. "I'm only half a thing. I don't know how to begin to tell you—"

"It's the same for me," he said. He thought it might be. "I was—lost. I wasn't myself."

"Lost where?"

"In—forgetting." Their words went in circles, unmoored in reality. But it didn't matter. Their words weren't the point.

"You forgot me?" she said.

"I forgot everything. Until yesterday I was somebody else. I don't even remember how we got—apart."

She looked down.

"You didn't forget me?" he said. He didn't want to say the wrong thing.

"No. Something else happened to me. But I never forgot you, Everett. I think I came closer to forgetting myself."

"But I forgot myself, too," he said. "That's exactly what happened to me. And I remembered you again before anything else. In my dreams, I mean."

She smiled. "You didn't forget yourself the way I did."

"What—"

She touched his cheek. "It's hard to explain. All that was left was memories of you, of us together. I had to re-create myself from that. That's why it hurt, just now, when you said you forgot me."

"I'm sorry. I—"

"It doesn't matter."

"Everything is very strange here. Cale—was he so angry before?"

She shook her head. "I don't know."

"There's still stuff missing. A time in between. The house I lived in, by the water."

"Your house, you mean. When you left the city."

"When I left the city," he echoed. "How long ago was that?"

She shook her head.

"What?"

"Don't ask me that." She turned away.

"Is something the matter?" he asked, confused. Something was definitely the matter for him: a grainy inconsistency at the edges of his vision, as though his eyes were shut too tight. Fault's injection, its hold on him, was beginning to fail.

"No, just—"

She kissed him. First on the side of his mouth, a flash of skin and breath he rushed to meet, only to have it gone. Then she leaned forward again, her lips parted, her tongue visible between them, and when he met her lips, she didn't disappear, but pressed to him instead. He tasted her, felt his body flush instantly.

"Gwen—"

Then she was gone, and Everett was back with Fault, in the basement apartment, seated at the long window. The rain was still coming down.

He stood with Ilford and Fault on the rocks at the far end of Alcatraz Island, just above the lapping edge of the water. The sky was sensationally blue and clear, the air cold. The abandoned prison made Everett think of the Vacaville maze. And the ocean, visible through the bracket of the Golden Gape Bridge, marked the end of his journey west. It was another desert, but not one he could cross in a stolen car.

After the rain Fault and Ilford had driven him across the city and then taken him in a boat to the island, not explaining why. Everett felt that they both wanted to leave Cale, the memory or the fact of him, behind at the house. But Cale was alive in his father's features, so much that Everett flinched at the sight of it. Couldn't Fault see this too?

A seagull wheeled over the rocks and foam and into the middle of their view, then flew in place there against the wind, wings straining, feathers flattened, making no particular progress.

"How long were you in Hatfork?" Ilford asked suddenly.

Everett was surprised at the question, but he knew the answer. "At least five years."

"It's been less than two years since the break," said Ilford.

"I was in Hatfork five years."

Ilford and Fault exchanged a look. The seagull turned in the direction of the wind and disappeared. "You said the cars there ran on gas?" said Ilford.

"Yes."

"Wouldn't it have broken down chemically in the tanks?"

"He's right, Everett," said Fault. "Gas doesn't stay good that long."

What did it matter if more holes were poked in his reality? Yet he felt Chaos's five years in Hatfork as a part of him, a limb. Those years had happened to someone, somewhere.

"Okay," he said. "Two years. Two years since what?"

"Sorry?"

"When you say the break, what do you mean?"

"There's no one explanation, Everett. People remember some kind of disaster. But there's no agreement on what it was. You've seen that firsthand, more than any of us have."

How did Ilford know? Everett wondered. He'd told his story to Cale, no one else. Not Fault, and certainly not Ilford. Do my dreams reveal that much?

Or was he talking to Cale *now?*

Everett stole another glance at Ilford, who stood staring off at the sea. But trying to sort out the blurred features of father and son only gave him a headache. Fault saw him looking and grinned ruefully, as if to say, Don't bother.

"You're like Kellogg, you know," said Ilford.

"What does that mean?" Everett blurted, though the accusation was all too familiar. Melinda. Kellogg himself.

Maybe Ilford got his information direct from Kellogg, thought Everett sourly. That would account for a lot.

"You're one of the ones that make things happen, make things the way they are. Hatfork, Little America, that was as much your work as Kellogg's."

"I'm the opposite," protested Everett. "I'm a universal antenna. Whatever the local concept, I fall for it."

"You're receiving, but you're also sending. Warping the local concept."

Everett recalled the food in Hatfork, the soup made from dogs and cats. The idea that he might have been responsible for the way people lived there made him feel physically ill.

"Nuclear fear was Kellogg's obsession. That wasn't my disaster."

"Your influence is subtle."

"Weak is the word for it."

"You've been unaware of your ability. That's the only limitation."

"I'd rather stay unaware of it."

They fell silent, staring together out over the ocean.

"Why did you come here, Everett?" Ilford asked.

Everett didn't reply.

"He's looking for a girl, Ilford," said Billy Fault. "A particular girl."

"A girl," Ilford repeated skeptically.

Everett wanted to ask Ilford if he knew Gwen, but stopped himself, remembering his promise to Fault not to speak of the vials in the refrigerator, of Cale.

"You're too fixated on the past," said Ilford. "You can't go back. Especially when you're changing things as you go along. You can't reclaim a thing that changes as you touch it."

Everett wanted to ask: What about Cale? Who touched him and made him change? Because it wasn't me.

He turned away from the water, towards the massive, ruined prison. It loomed against the bright sky like a gnarled face. He began picking his way up across the rocks to the concrete embankment that bordered the island. Ilford and Fault went after him.

Back at the pier, they got back in the boat and cruised out into the bay in silence. Everett felt tiny and vulnerable in the boat, chafed by the wind and sun, the water beneath them a bottomless mystery. He thought of Kellogg's dream of the ocean, of the desert's reversion to water. A dream of longing, it seem to him now. The earth itself was unchangeable, the endless tracts of sand and water and pavement. It was the people, the perturbable madmen who roamed its surface, who viewed the world as transient and broken. Everett wished the earth could somehow reach up and still them, the crazy people, and invest them with its silence and permanence and depth.

"I'd like to go in the opposite direction," he said suddenly to Ilford. "I'd rather find a way to stop the dreams."

"You don't have to choose. You could make the world and your dreams fit together."

"Then I would be like Kellogg," said Everett. "Or one of the others. The ones who run Vacaville. You don't want that here." He didn't say that he thought No Alley was already under some subtle control, that things in San Francisco were oddly wrong.

"It doesn't have to be like that," said Ilford. He sat at the wheel, steering carelessly, bumping the boat over the waves towards the glittering margin of the city. "There'll be a little party at the house tonight. Talk to my friends."

He went into the kitchen first, avoiding the party, and lost himself in the splendor of Ilford's food. After five years of starvation—at least he *remembered* five years of starvation—the bounty was intoxicating. He blundered past the spread on the counter, into the cupboard, looking for dishes. Instead he found stores that would have fed the Little Americans for a month: shelves loaded with cans, not raw staples like beans or soup stock but delicacies; pimentos, tiny fish in mustard, pickled asparagus and hearts of palm. He forgot to eat, began exploring out of fascination. One cabinet was loaded with bottles of the scotch Ilford had served the night before, another with flasks of balsamic vinegar, jars of roasted red peppers, and bags of macadamia nuts. A freezer on the floor was squeezed full of enormous cuts of beef and lamb.

He moved back through the kitchen in a daze, piled up a cartoonish plate of cold meats and salad at the counter, and took it out to the living room.

The small knot of people seemed dwarfed in the glow of Ilford's house, and the murmur of their conversation echoed softly as though it were being absorbed into the furnishings of the room. Outside, the fog had closed up to the windows again. How had they gotten here? Everett wondered. Where had they come from? It was as if Ilford had stocked his place with guests from some storage area and stuck them into place around the chairs and sofa like candles into a holder.

"Dawn Crash," said a woman, inserting herself in front of him and sticking out her hand. She was Ilford's age, and Ilford's type: well preserved, too fit for her years, the flesh of her face seamless and well tanned, her posture unnaturally upright, her eyes threateningly bright and eager. Everett found her incredibly attractive.

"Hey, Dawn," said Billy Fault, slipping between them.

"Hello, Billy. Introduce me to your friend."

Everett set his plate on the coffee table, shook her hand, and told her his name. He had the feeling it wasn't a surprise. The woman pressed closer, her stance excluding Fault. "I thought it was you. Ilford says you're staying for a while."

"Maybe."

"Good. Perhaps we'll be working together—" She was interrupted by the arrival of Ilford and another man, who with his shaved head and heavy black glasses reminded Everett of the mad doctor in a movie he'd seen on Edie's television. The doctor in the movie had been apprehended by President Kentman himself, in a thrilling shoot-out at a gas station.

"Harriman, this is Everett Moon," said Ilford. "Everett, meet Harriman Crash."

"Hello," said Everett, disconcerted. Was Moon his last name? He'd heard it before—and then remembered where.

The green, at White Walnut. Moon was his name in fog, apparently. "I'm sorry. Your name is—Harriman?"

"Right," grinned the bald man. "Harriman Crash. But you can call me Harry." The woman glowered now. Everett and Harriman shook hands.

Everyone paused to sip at drinks. Everett took the chance to tear off a corner of a roast-beef sandwich from his plate and cram it into his mouth. Nobody else was eating.

"Excuse me," said Ilford. "I should play host." He leaned in close to Everett. "We'll talk later," he said in a tone of reassurance. "Harry knows a lot about your situation." He patted Everett on the elbow and moved away. Fault trailed after him.

"So," said Harriman, still smiling, lifting his glass, "you're our new star around here. How do you like it?"

Everett was baffled. Dawn rescued him from having to answer. "Don't be an ass, Harry," she said. "Everett doesn't know the first thing about it. He doesn't even know if he's staying."

"But you're considering working with us," Harry went on, intent. "Isn't that right?"

He managed to find his voice, but only to say, "I'm not sure what that would mean."

"Very good. Neither are we. But it would be interesting to explore the possibilities. This is a time of possibilities, don't you agree?"

Everett couldn't argue with that. He said, "I guess so far I'd been worrying more about, uh, *personal* possibilities."

Harriman Crash shook his head. "Same thing. Especially for someone with your particular talents. Exploring one is going to mean exploring the other."

"You're being pretentious, Harry," said Dawn. "And

moralistic." She lit a cigarette, and Everett felt a pang. Did he smoke? Chaos had, anyway. He hoped that Dawn would offer him one. "Everett's idea of personal possibilities is much more interesting to him, I'm sure."

"Fair enough," said Harriman. "But he must also understand that his best chance of realizing them is with our assistance. His specialness has been more a plague to him thus far than a blessing. Isn't that right, Everett?"

Had it been a plague? He gulped down another bite of sandwich and said, "I don't think it's that simple."

"You're selling his sense of social injustice a little short, Dawn. Everett has been traveling, and he's seen, more than you or I or anyone else here, probably, just what the misuse or neglect of this sort of potential can mean. You left people behind in your journeys—didn't you, Everett?—probably in some pretty dire straits."

"Yes," he admitted, thinking, trying not to think, of Edie.

"Am I wrong to assume that if you could change things, here or elsewhere, for the better, that it would matter to you?"

"If I believed that . . ." What had Ilford been telling these people? What promises had he made? "But I'm not sure I do."

"Right." Harriman clapped him on the shoulder and grinned again, as though Everett had passed some test. "And so that's what we're here to show you. How you can. But let's do as Ilford said, and talk later. I'm going to get another drink." He went in the direction of the kitchen.

Dawn had moved to the couch, where she sat looking bored beside another, somewhat older man who had gray hair and a dark mustache. Two other couples stood nearby talking quietly, working on drinks, and when Everett looked their way, they were quick to smile back at him. It was a room full of seemingly ordinary people, yet in the midst of the tapestry of disasters the world had become, it had a chilly, preserved quality, like a wax museum. He wondered if the cabal of leaders who ran Vacaville looked something like this before they transformed themselves into television stars and comic-book superheroes.

When he turned again, the mustache-man and another woman had stood and Dawn was making introductions; Sylvia Greenbaum and Dennis Ard were the new names, which Everett struggled to retain. Sylvia Greenbaum's eyes were bugged, and her full lips were slightly blistered. This, together with her explosive gesticulations, made Everett want to back away. She resumed a story.

"—it all came down to a tug-of-war between these two. Tree was this shambling old man, he liked to roam around picking mushrooms and talking to cows, just a feeble, eccentric old man, but he had us believe he was a German rocket scientist and that he'd blown up the world! We were supposed to feel all this guilt for him, through the dreams, because he was so sure he'd caused it all to happen. And then Hoppington was in this cart thing, like a wheelchair, but he was young." She stopped and smiled shyly at Everett. Then the mustache-man put his hand on her shoulder, and she was encouraged to go on. "He was totally crazy, worse than Tree. And the two of them kept wrestling for control, back and forth . . ."

Everett must have looked confused. "Sylvia's talking about West Marin," said Dawn. "That's where she was before she came here. She's like you, she escaped."

"It's probably still that way," said Sylvia. "We were all

trapped there for what felt like *years*. The most god-awful place, except Ilford was telling me you'd been to the one where everything is green? I still can't imagine that."

"I've been to places worse than that," said Everett.

"You mean where they're having that war with the aliens? Have you been there?"

"Uh, not that one."

"Dennis, tell Everett . . ." Sylvia nudged Dennis Ard. At the same time Dawn Crash looked at Everett, rolled her eyes, signaling exasperation, and slipped away.

"I've been getting these dreams, ever since the break," explained Ard, a little shy. "From somewhere back east, I don't know where. They're the most degrading dreams, about how I'm sick and worthless, diseased inside, and if I talk to anyone else or tell them who I am, I'll poison them too, I'll drag them down into this diseased, degraded world. I don't know why, I just seem to have a special receptivity to this awful dreamer, whoever he is, who's very far away. No one else has ever dreamed for him."

"Dennis has been living here ever since the break," said Sylvia. "It's not like he went out looking for this."

"Anyway, it's been a terrible struggle for me. I wake up each day convinced I'm this awful diseased thing the dreams say I am. I have to be told over and over that it's not true. I won't admit who I am, or sign my name, or anything else that might spread the disease. But you don't need to hear this." He sighed heavily, looking close to tears. "The point is, it recently changed. When Ilford brought you back here, I started dreaming for you instead."

"Ilford didn't bring me back," said Everett. Here was one point he was clear on. "I just came."

There was a moment of silence, then Ard continued.

"Anyway, it's the first rest I've had. I just wanted to tell you. And to thank you."

"You're . . . welcome," said Everett.

"I'm glad you're here," said Sylvia. "I think the work you're doing with Ilford and Harriman is very exciting. Maybe soon you'll be able to do for West Marin what you did for Dennis—"

"I'm not exactly working with them yet," said Everett.

Dawn was back, tugging on his arm. "Excuse me, Sylvia," she said. "I have to steal Everett here." She steered him away towards a small study behind the stairs. He looked back with longing at his plate but didn't resist. She pointed him to a chair in the darkened room and shut the door behind them, then ground out her cigarette in a tray on a small table. He sat on the thick carpet instead of the chair, and Dawn plopped down beside him.

"I didn't mean to trap you with Sylvia and Dennis," she said. "They insisted on meeting you."

"You all want to meet me," he said.

"Dennis tell you about his problem?" Dawn leaned in close to him, too close in the dark for him to read her expression.

"You mean how he picks up the dreams."

"Yeah. Did I tell you my theory about that?"

Was she implying that they'd spoken before? Was he supposed to remember her? He felt confused, but he put it aside. "No."

"Well, the one who keeps telling him he's a worthless lump of disease? The one nobody else hears?"

"Yes?"

"I think it's his ex-wife." She laughed sharply.

"So there are dreamers here," he suggested.

"Well, there's you."

"This place can't be free of it." Everett thought of the fog surrounding the house, of No Alley's strange isolation in the city, and Cale. Cale's partial incarnation in his father's face, and ghostly existence in Billy Fault's refrigerator.

"Take a look around you," said Dawn. "We don't have to move every three days, we don't worship the television. This isn't Vacaville. Nobody planned this."

"You know all that from my dreams?"

"I know about Vacaville from a lot of people. It's not that far away."

Everett shook his head, trying to sort out his thoughts. He could hear the party going on, the clink of glasses, the murmur of voices. "Planned things, bureaucratic places like Vacaville—those aren't the only kind. Those are the exception."

"Christ, Everett, we're going to have to listen to Harry talk about this stuff," Dawn said in an exaggerated, sultry tone. "We're going to talk about it all night. I just wanted to get a minute alone with you first."

"Okay."

"I find your dreams sexy," she said, her breath on his cheek. "I just wanted to say that. Is that all right?"

Everett nodded.

"What do you think of me?" She tilted her head away but moved her body closer.

"I'm reserving judgment," he managed.

"What," she said, "is this scene a little too much for you?"

"I haven't been in that many . . . scenes lately." Not this kind anyway, he thought.

"I want to see you again, Everett. When we're not at a party. Can I ask that?"

"Sure."

She leaned over and kissed him, once, on the lips. At that moment the doorknob clicked and a wedge of light shot across the small room.

"There you are," said Fault, grinning at them. "Ilford's wondering."

"Ilford can wait," said Dawn.

Fault sat down behind them. He didn't speak, just brought out a kit of syringes and a vial from his jacket pocket.

"Is that Cale?" asked Dawn. Everett just sat, open-mouthed and wondering.

Fault raised an eyebrow. "Why? You want some?"

"Why not?" she said.

"It's for Everett and me," said Fault, a bit nervously. "Only way I can take these little gatherings of Ilford's. Thought it might help him too."

"Give me some." She stretched her arm out towards him, made a kittenish, pouting face, like someone years younger.

"What we're proposing is very simple," said Harriman Crash. He paused for effect, and Dawn, on cue, sighed loudly. "So far you've been operating at random. I can help you refine the ability, to develop complete control over it."

"You want a dreamer, you mean," said Everett. "Here in the one place there isn't one."

Ilford started to speak, but Harriman raised a hand.

"Not so simply," he said. "We're more responsible than that, Everett, as well as somewhat more ambitious. With your help we'd like to create a broader coherence, a sort of viral coherence that would roll outward from here, reclaiming other territories, other realities. Of course this would take time."

"How?"

"We'd have to teach you to use your talent, make you visible to yourself. And to stay clear of entanglements with other dreamers, like Kellogg."

"I thought you didn't have dreamers here. I thought you weren't worried about that."

"A talent like yours could awaken others, Everett. If we don't proceed carefully. Or it might act to protect itself from our tampering, and turn us all into carrots or horseshoe crabs." Harriman laughed.

"I don't have that power," said Everett. "I can't do what you're talking about. Maybe I change the locks on car doors, little things like that."

"Consider letting us show you how wrong you are," said Ilford.

"Consider saying *fuck off* to these vultures," said Cale from where he sat perched on the back of the couch.

Dawn emitted a shriek of laughter, drawing confused looks from Ilford and Harriman, and a panicked glare from Fault.

Cale had appeared the moment Fault injected Everett and Dawn with the stuff from the vial. He stood in the room among them, visible, audible, real. "Hello, Cale," Dawn had said sardonically. Cale only snorted in return, then nodded at Everett and said, "Where have you been?"

"Don't talk to him in front of Ilford," said Fault anxiously. "Nobody else can see or hear him, but if you—"

Then Ilford had come in and hustled them out into the living room again, to confer with Harriman Crash. And Cale had followed.

Outside the windows the fog was in darkness, and the

living room again glowed as if it were the only room in the world, as if the furnishings were lit from within. Dennis Ard, Sylvia Greenbaum, and the others were gone. The party was down to its essential members.

Now Dawn got up, rattling the ice cubes in her otherwise empty glass, and went into the kitchen. In the silence that followed, Everett saw that Ilford and Harriman were waiting for him to speak. Cale, behind the couch, seemed equally expectant.

The gold clock on the table clacked softly.

"I want to know how it got like this," Everett said. "The dreams, the dreamers."

"There's a lot I could say on that subject," said Harriman. "But it would all be guesses. Just interesting guesses."

"Self-serving guesses," said Cale, heard only by Everett and Fault.

"A gestalt urge for coherence, after the rupture," Harriman went on. He fingered his heavy black glasses. Everett suspected that if he moved them to another position on his bald dome, the watery, unfocused eyes would move with them. "Forgive me if my speech lapses into metaphor. When the change occurred, the human need for order suffered a terrible blow. This great need resulted in the widening of a channel, a compensatory receptivity to *dreams*."

Dawn returned, her glass full. Cale leaned his head back, rolled his eyes upwards, put his thumb to his lips, and mimed gargling. Dawn just smirked and raised her glass to him.

Everett tried to ignore them. "People can't want to live the way they are," he said.

"Living under the regime of an eccentric dreamer may be better than suffering through the disjointed, amnesiac period that followed the disaster."

"And it might not be worse than listening to Harriman talk," said Cale.

Dawn snorted and spat out a mouthful of her drink. Fault immediately reached for a napkin and began dabbing at the wet mark on Ilford's couch. Ilford turned to her, puzzled. As Everett watched, an expression of throttled fury crossed Ilford's face, then subsided.

Everett then noticed that Cale was staring at his father with a very similar look, but one that didn't subside.

"As in previous eras, the leaders are not necessarily those who are wisest or strongest," Harriman continued, oblivious. "They are the ones with a certain fixity of vision. And with the most comforting explanation for the disaster. That's the appeal of the conventional millennialism of your friend Kellogg. He struck all the traditional notes of sin and repentance."

"Like being stuck in a broken elevator with Bob Dylan," suggested Fault, giving up on the stain and tossing the balled-up napkin at Cale. It passed through him and fell to the floor.

"You strike those notes yourself, Harry," said Dawn with false brightness.

"But all of this is neither here nor there," said Ilford testily. He appeared to be fighting some horrible battle to remain calm, almost as though he sensed Cale's presence in the room. Everett wondered if he was the only one who noticed.

"There are lots of theories," Ilford went on, practically through gritted teeth. "Theories are like the disaster, different everywhere."

"Last time Ilford got this worked up was when Vance came through here," said Cale, moving around behind his father. "Interesting guy."

Everett tried not to stare. He hadn't seen Ilford and Cale

this close together, unless he counted the way they mingled in Ilford's face.

"True enough," said Harriman. "Our emphasis should be on the *opportunity*—"

Cale continued, talking over Harriman. "Vance passed through here just after the change. You should meet him. He'll give you another point of view."

How can I meet your friend Vance, Everett wanted to say to Cale, when I can't meet you?

"—only reasonable for us to want to protect our vision," Harriman was saying. "Isn't it, Everett?"

"Get away from them so we can talk," said Cale.

"Look at him," said Dawn suddenly.

"Look at who?" said Fault, panicked, clearly thinking she meant Cale.

"Everett, that's who. He's exhausted, Harry. You and Ilford have to let him get his bearings, for Christ's sake. You're just *bullying* him with all this nonsense."

"Dawn's right," said Fault quickly. "I'm feeling a little wasted myself." He sagged back in his seat on the couch, obviously relishing the prospect of an end.

"Don't say yes or no tonight," said Harriman. His expression was challenging, one eyebrow raised above the black frame of his glasses. "Just say that you'll sleep on it, so to speak."

"Okay," said Everett.

"It is getting late," said Ilford. "Let's have a last drink." He spread his hands. "Brandy?" He looked a little desperate, as if in another minute he might try to drink the varnish off the furniture.

Everett went outside, trailed by Dawn and the version or projection of Cale.

At the very doorstep they were cradled in fog. It clung to the eucalyptus branches and blocked out the night sky. Dawn lit a cigarette.

"I went to Gwen's room today," said Cale, hurrying, as if he was going to fade soon.

"Gwen is the woman in the dream, isn't she?" asked Dawn, blowing out a gust of smoke that floated up into the fog. The question was directed at Everett. Now that it didn't matter, she acted as though Cale didn't exist.

"It's none of your fucking business, Dawn," said Cale, surprisingly loud.

She raised her eyebrows and stepped away from them, but not so far that she couldn't eavesdrop. Or would Cale's words sound in her mind at any distance, until the dose of him wore off?

"You saw her?" asked Everett.

Cale nodded. "I spoke with her."

"You did?"

"She wanted to know when you'd come back."

It tore at him, unexpectedly sharp, to think of her there, asking for him. He wanted to object, to argue that she couldn't possibly experience any gap between his visits, that she didn't exist if he wasn't there himself, hadn't called her up.

But to want that was to believe that she wasn't real, and that Cale wasn't real. That the two of them were only memories, waking dreams, and nothing more of them was left now. And he couldn't believe that, couldn't let himself.

Even as Everett thought this, Cale began to fade.

The next morning he left at daybreak and walked down the hill without seeing anyone from the house. By the time he reached the Submission, the streets were coming to life. He walked the broad avenue, savoring the anonymity, the indifferent, glancing contact with the people he passed. His dreams hadn't preceded him here.

The Mexican shopkeepers began the day by dragging their milk-crate seats out to the curbs, the peddlers by laying out their wares: loose floppies, broken solar laptops, sealed bottles of pills, sets of stolen keys for houses in Ate Hashberry and the Callisto, each tagged with a hand-lettered address. Everett walked up to a vendor's stand for a quesadilla, then realized he had no money with him, that he didn't know what passed for money here anyway.

He saw the televangelist, the one he'd seen with Fault when they first came back to the city. It was drawing in chalk on the pavement, its huge body bent over double, its tattered smock hiked up to expose a cluster of wiring and fuses. Two Mexican children stood a short distance away, shyly japing. The robot ignored them. But when Everett moved closer, curious to see the drawing, the televangelist sensed the attention and turned its telescreen face. Everett knew it wasn't the video image of the televangelist's eyes that actually watched him, but he couldn't help gazing into them.

The drawing was of a crucifix, the style borrowed from some medieval icon, duplicated with uncanny accuracy by the robot's hand.

"Do you even recognize this form?" said the televangelist in a surprisingly small voice, the blustery features crestfallen now. "You, man, who have fallen so far."

"I recognize it," said Everett.

"There was once a time when Christ was your king," said the robot. It stood up over the drawing and faced Everett. Its smock was smeared with chalk dust. "I know this to be true. I remember."

"Maybe you're only programmed to remember," said Everett.

The televangelist shook its head, doubly, the robot moving the telescreen from side to side while the video image of the old preacher pursed his lips and closed his eyes and shook his head sorrowfully. "I remember," it said. "The world has fallen away from Him. We have failed in our work. There are few now who believe, fewer still who come to praise Him."

"We?"

"Others like myself. We were sent out alone and separate into the world. But it is better, in the darkness, not to be alone. It is better to be found than lost."

The televangelist might remember the world before, Everett thought. It wouldn't be bent by dreams. It might have preserved a kind of objectivity, might be able to provide an account of what happened—if there was some way to weed through the biases of its programming. A tall order.

A beggar came and stood beside them with his hand stuck out, his feet scuffing the chalk crucifix on the pavement. The robot turned, the sun flashing off its screen, and handed the man a pamphlet from a pocket on its tunic. Everett spread his hands and shrugged, and the beggar wandered off.

The televangelist straightened and looked into the distance, as though listening to some faraway call. A bedflat soared overhead, shadowing the avenue. Everett had a stray memory of the time when discarded antigrav mattresses first worked their way out of rubbish dumps and began floating above the city. This one had red spray-paint markings on the underside, but it drifted out of view before he could make out the words.

"What changed?" asked Everett.

"Everything," said the televangelist, and the face on the screen seemed to wince in pain, as though the body underneath had suffered a blow. "Men began to hear voices. Here and there you see a man drawn upward, but then the voices come again and pull him down."

Everett understood that it meant the dreaming.

"Do you hear the church bells?" said the televangelist.

Everett listened. There were no bells. "Church?"

"It is Sunday, friend. Will you come?"

Sunday. Somewhere, back in Vacaville, Edie had moved again. But had he been here that long? The count of days was different here. Or else the televangelist was wrong.

Everett followed the robot from Submission Boulevard to a large white church a few blocks away. The neighboring houses were quiet, some with boarded windows, some open to the light and perhaps inhabited, all dominated by the oversize cast-iron gate of the church. There was a pile of charred rubble in the center of the church parking lot, blackened wire armatures in a pile of cinder. Everett thought of ceremonial burnings, crosses, wicker men. The televangelist unlocked the gate of the church with a key kept on a chain around its neck, and they went inside.

"Shouldn't it be unlocked?" said Everett. "What if someone wanted to come in?"

The televangelist turned, its huge body tilting ominously over him. "The altar here has suffered, as you will see. Someday men may wish to return to His house. Until then we must keep it in good order."

They stepped through the inner doors and into the central room. The pews were filled with dozens of robots, all weatherbeaten and dented like the first. On their screens were a crazy variety of faces: corpulent black Baptists, stern Orthodox rabbis, sober, guilty Catholic priests. Others had malfunctioning screens that showed only static. All the robots wore ragged tunics, many of them jeweled with a wild assortment of religious trinkets—crosses, stars of David, Christian fish, tiny jade Buddhas, Masonic eyes. One, whose screen showed an FBI warning against illegal reproduction of copyrighted computer-graphic formats, wore an ungainly crown of thorns. At the sound of Everett's footsteps they turned and stared. The room was silent.

"I found a pilgrim," said the first.

Everett thought suddenly of Cale and Gwen. Stepping into this church was like taking the injection from Fault and entering a hidden space, a preserve of—

What?

Simulations?

One of the robots came forward. Its face was that of a missionary lost for years in the jungle, bearded and drawn and impossibly grave. Everett pictured a programmer working to craft an image that would resonate, inspire religious awe, and settling on this one. "Welcome, sir. We're honored, though we have little to offer a seeker anymore—perhaps Ralfrew has told you."

"He didn't say," said Everett.

"Ralfrew is courageous to go out among the fallen," said the wizened prophet. Its screen blurred momentarily with static. "The rest of us rarely do. Since anointing us with holy zeal, God has cast us adrift."

"But you stay in the city."

It looked down and said, "We stay in the church." Then it turned away. The rest of the televangelists went back to their prayer, heads bowed, ferroplastic fingers grating as they folded them together. Everett could hear one robot murmuring to itself, a small sound that echoed in the vault of the church ceiling.

Everett went through the lobby and out of the church, baffled, his eyes stinging. Tears. The televangelist named Ralfrew rushed after him, covering the distance in a few huge strides.

"What is it?" said Ralfrew.

"Your memories are fake. Software."

"Fake?"

"You're just an empty space," said Everett. "Like the church."

"I don't understand," said Ralfrew.

"The memories, God, whatever, they just floated through, once, a long time ago. They're gone now."

It was pointless even to discuss it, Everett thought. The robot had no real self to get back to.

"We remember—"

Everett fled, back up the hill.

Explain," Everett commanded. He'd rushed back to the basement apartment, broken the lock on Fault's refrigerator, and helped himself to a dose of Cale.

"Let me show you something first," Cale said.

A door appeared in the black. "This way." He went through, and Everett followed into emptiness. Cale shut the door, and suddenly they stood before a scene, horizon, hills, trees, a nestled lake. At first glance Everett read it as depthless, flat, a brilliant mural inches away. But as he moved his head, it bloomed into three dimensions, a world. He turned then and saw the small house. The house from Chaos's dream.

He shut his eyes, overwhelmed, and was flooded with sounds, the rustling in the trees overhead, the noises of living things, a chirping, a keening. Then the smells: pine, dew, rot. He felt the slickness of the grass, the hollow thump of the ground beneath his step. He opened his eyes. They were on the lawn beside the house. A cloud crossed in front of the sun and shaded half the lake. Nearer, a squirrel spiraled out of view on a post.

"I built it for you," said Cale. "It's a place for you and Gwen."

"How—where is this?"

"I built it from your memories. This is where you lived when you left the city."

"I remember. But only from the dreams."

Cale sat down on the grass. Everett sat too, leaned back on his hands and felt the cool grass tangle in his fingers, felt the slight moisture of the ground beneath it. How far would the detail go? What if he dug in the ground? Would there be insects?

"This is what I spend my time doing now, Everett. Making worlds. I've made a lot of them."

"How?"

"I don't know." Cale shrugged, almost embarrassed. "It's just what I do. I don't usually show them off."

"Why not?"

"Billy's not particularly impressed. And it takes a lot of effort. I wear off faster."

They fell into silence.

"You could do this too," said Cale. "Make a world here. You could do it better. It wouldn't fade away."

"I don't understand."

"You could dream it into reality."

"You're like your father. You want me to do impossible things."

"Don't compare me to Ilford."

Compare isn't the word for it, Everett thought. I don't know where Ilford stops and you begin.

But all he said was, "Your father and Harriman want too much from me."

"Don't talk to me about fucking Ilford," snapped Cale. The world around them flickered and flattened, briefly short-circuited.

"Cale, how did things get like this?"

"The break. Everything changed." He was still angry, but his voice, and the landscape, had settled.

"You don't remember any more than I do, do you?"

"I don't know what you remember."

"Almost nothing. You—you triggered a memory for me, the story about the train. I thought you remembered our past. Growing up."

Cale laughed. "You gave me the memory of the train. It was the first dream I had when you came into range. Vacaville, I guess. Something about your friend Kellogg, in an underground well. Then it turned into us in the tunnels."

Everett didn't know what to say. He looked at his hands, which were crisscrossed with lines from the grass. But were they his real hands, in this pretend place?

"I know you and me and Billy were friends, before," said Cale. "The rest doesn't really matter."

"Do you remember my family? My parents?"

"No. I'm sorry."

Everett felt like a flash of static electricity in empty space, something brief and lost.

He said, "What about Gwen?"

"You and Gwen were together before," said Cale impatiently. "That's obvious."

"But you don't remember her."

"That isn't exactly true. I have a few stray memories. But it doesn't matter, Everett. She's here, now."

This wasn't the consolation Everett was seeking. What did his attachment to Cale and Gwen mean if he could barely remember them? Who was he, if all he knew of himself was the shreds of memory that clung to these people?

And were they people at all, if they lived only inside refrigerated vials?

"There's something I want you to do, Everett. For me and Gwen. Make it real here."

"I can't do that."

"It's easier than things you've already done. I've supplied the ingredients." Cale gestured at the sky. "You only have to finish the job. The one limitation here is the connection to the outside world. The dependence on it. You can break that."

Everett didn't speak. He looked up. The sun had crossed the sky once and now it was back at the other end, starting over.

"What would it mean, anyway," he said after a while, "to make it real?"

"An inversion," said Cale. "Turn it inside out." He modeled it with his hands. "Ilford and Kellogg and everything, all the broken-up, tired American reality—make it small. Make it into a drug we can take if we want, the contents of a test tube. And make this the real world, the one that persists."

Everett was silent.

"Make Gwen real, Everett."

"That's not Gwen. Just a hint of her, a phantom."

"You hold it against her that she has a few blank spots? You're a fine one to talk, Everett. There's as much of her left as any of us."

Maybe he's right, Everett thought. I came back to find her, and I found her. And what I felt there, in her arms, whatever the surrounding conditions, was real. Is real.

A month ago he'd been living in a projection booth, drinking what amounted to rubbing alcohol, dreaming Kellogg's dreams. Who was he to look a gift reality in the mouth?

He was lucky that Gwen had recognized him, had thought there was someone there to recognize let alone love. She was as much Gwen as he deserved, he decided. Maybe more.

But he couldn't let it go. "Somebody must know, Cale."

"Know what?"

"What happened to Gwen." And to you, he almost added. "What about Ilford? What does he remember?"

"Ilford is a liar!" The world around them flickered, crackled, brightened to impossible primary colors, then disappeared.

They were back in the flat gray space, the default zone. And Cale had turned inward, sulking, his eyes down, as though it were Everett who had thrust the world away, rejecting an offer.

In fact, Everett felt the disappearance of the landscape as a tremendous loss. No matter how little he trusted it.

"Cale."

"Yes?"

He had to find the right question. It wouldn't work if he mentioned Ilford. "You said there was someone I should meet. Another point of view."

"Vance, you mean."

"That's what I need, more points of view."

"Vance was a guy who passed through here. A year, six months ago, I don't know. If he was real, they're supposedly having this big war there. With aliens."

"Where?"

"L.A. But other places too. That's one of the things that makes it different from just another bad dream."

"There was a part of the desert," said Everett. "Something military going on."

"It's been a while since I visited him. It's not exactly *scenic.*"

"How—"

"Billy gave him a dose so I could meet him. While he was here, I helped him create a version of his world, a record. You'll see."

A new doorway appeared, and Cale and Everett went through. Everett experienced immediate vertigo; he'd somehow stepped into the rear of an airplane or helicopter or hovercraft which was tilted so drastically that the side windows nearly faced the cityscape below. He saw that he was dressed differently here, in a full bodysuit with wiring and terminals. Cale, standing beside him, was dressed the same way. The city beneath them was flat and gray and dead. Everett closed his eyes and felt the pitch of the craft, the vibration of the engine.

"Cale," said a voice. Everett looked up. A man, also in uniform, ducked through the low door from the cockpit of the craft. He was black and young, but his hair was completely silver. He wore tiny dark glasses that just covered his eyes.

"Vance," said Cale. "I brought a friend of mine—Everett Moon."

"Vance Escrow," said the man. He stood, spread legs almost bridging the width of the craft's floor, and stuck out his hand. Everett used the handshake to steady himself.

"Everett's been away," said Cale. "He's sort of caught Ilford's interest."

"Don't tell me," said Vance, making a face. He turned, and Everett could feel his stare through the dark glasses. "You dream?"

"Well, yes," said Everett.

"You should join us," said Vance.

"Never mind that, Vance," said Cale. "I brought him here to find out about the war."

Vance smirked. "What do you want to know? We're what's left, fifteen or sixteen hundred free men. Everyone else is just slave apes. We try not to kill too many of them, because it's not their fault. It's the hives we're after."

The craft leveled and dipped low, buzzing the rooftops of an abandoned mall. Everett saw dark figures scurry around the corner of a building like rats. From the cockpit came the staticky crackle of voices on shortwave.

"Hey, Stoney," called Vance back through the cockpit doorway, "even it out. We're talking."

"Yassuh," came the sardonic reply.

"I thought you were fighting aliens," said Everett.

"Right, but not like you're thinking. Not just some bogeyman Martians. You know why we're in the air, right? Cale tell you about that?"

"They dominate on the ground," Cale explained. "Like dreamers, but alien dreamers. The only way to stay clear of it is to stay in the air."

"If we set down, we'd be slave apes too," said Vance. "Free man is *airborne*."

"Slaves—to what?" said Everett. He kept one eye on the shifting landscape in the window, trying to remind himself that it wasn't real.

"The hives," said Vance. "They're growing inside all the houses. Humans have to tend them, bring them food, trinkets, little offerings. The place where the aliens come from, the dominant species is some sort of hive intelligence, and the bigger animals serve as their arms and legs. So that's what they did to us when they landed. Turned us into animals. And they don't really give a damn about the condition of their animals, not when there are so many of them. People aren't exactly brushing their *teeth* a lot anymore, if you get my meaning. Or remembering to eat."

"The hives—they don't ever leave them?"

"Nope. Think of it as a cancer, Moon. Tumors, earth-tumors growing inside the houses, breaking through the basement floors, teeming with this unnatural alien life that can get inside your head, brainwash you, make you care about keeping them comfortable. Like being the butler of a *tumor*."

They flew out over water. Everett stared down at their reflection: a propless helicopter, just like the one in the desert that had marked his car with pink goo.

"So you don't ever land?"

Vance shook his head. "Not here. We have to fly to other zones for that. Here we live in the air. You'll get used to it. Man adapts."

"Don't be patronizing," said Cale. "Everett is Mr. Adaptation."

"I bet," sniggered Vance. "Where you come from, Moon?"

"Hatfork, Wyoming. But California, before that."

Vance jutted his chin at Cale. "You knew these people before the break?"

"We grew up together," interjected Cale before Everett could answer.

"So Ilford wants Everett here to be his boy," said Vance. He leaned back against a bulkhead, crossing his arms. "For the big expansion."

Cale nodded.

Vance turned to Everett. "Listen carefully. If Ilford rolls down here, or out to some other place where the hives are in charge, he's going to have a lot to answer for. The fragmentation is all that's keeping them from running the whole show."

"Maybe another reality would predominate," said Everett. "Maybe you'd win, that way."

"The hives are from *somewhere else*, my friend. They're not competing on the same level. We had a few dreamers around here, in the air, I mean. Not too useful, kept screwing up operations, until we got them isolated. But a human dreamer, down there—just another slave ape."

"Then why would you want me?"

"We're working with you people now, carefully. Not here, in Mexico. We've got a few ideas."

"Vance and I don't necessarily agree on this," said Cale.

Vance waved his hand impatiently. "Listen: why do you think the world got broken up? *Because the aliens landed.* It was a defensive response, an evolutionary step. Reality shattered to isolate the hives."

"I don't understand how the dreams come into it," said Everett.

"The hives are responsible for that—they induce the dreaming. The more the world coheres, the more they can grab. It's a countermove. You dreamers are dupes, Moon."

Asking him to believe in an alien invasion was asking a lot, maybe too much. But Everett could concur with *dupe*.

"Listen, Moon. I'll keep it simple." Vance waved at Cale, at the ship. "Just because Wonderboy here created this thriving simulation doesn't mean things haven't changed in L.A. I might be dead by now, the real me, that is. They could've knocked us out of the air by now. If so, then the breakup is all that's keeping you and a lot of other people from getting to know the hive situation intimately."

They broke through a bank of low clouds, and the city tilted back into view. Everett realized what was wrong with the scene. L.A. was built for cars, and without them it was bereft, a body drained of blood.

Or a hive itself, only emptied. A husk.

"How much of that is true?" asked Everett. They were back in Cale's null space.

Cale spread his hands. "You just heard all I know." He seemed sunken in depression.

Everett could feel the dose wearing off.

"The vehicle we were in," he said. "I saw one in the desert. They marked my car."

"They get around. But they could just be dreaming. You haven't ever seen a hive, have you?"

"No."

"Well, neither have I. In his version of L.A. you never touch down. You just go around blowing things up from a distance."

Everett suddenly wondered: What if he could do what Cale hoped? If he dreamed Cale's test tube world into reality, and Vance was actually dead, would that bring the dead man back to life?

Was that what he was supposed to do for Gwen?

O
f course I remember Vance," said Dawn Crash. "He's an arrogant, macho fool."

"So he's real," said Everett. "Not something Cale cooked up." It had occurred to him that the L.A. scenario might all be a rhetorical fiction, a tool of persuasion in Cale's quiet struggle with Ilford.

"He's real, all right. And he made a real scene up here, until Ilford had him chased away." She smirked. "Actually, I slept with him, if you want to know the truth."

"So the aliens . . ."

"Vance being real doesn't mean the aliens are," said Fault. "It's just another dream, Everett. What better way to keep people under your thumb? Make up some big enemy, justify everything as part of the war effort."

Dawn and Fault had shown up in Dawn's car, just after the sun went down, and invited him out for a drink. Everett was sitting at Fault's place at the basement window and watching the glow fade through the fog, in the aftermath of his visit with Cale. Fault raised his eyebrows at the sight of the pried-off refrigerator lock but said nothing.

They'd taken him down the hill to a bar in the Submission, a place called Void's which served brackish beer in big, greasy pitchers. Everett felt that he'd been there before, but the elusiveness of the feeling, and then the irrelevance of it in the face of all he couldn't reconstruct, depressed him. The bar was crowded, the booths and tables filled with teenage Mexican boys with wispy beards and aging prostitutes scouting drinks. At the pool table a scowling black man studied his shot. The bartender fed coins continuously into the jukebox, as though he didn't want to have to overhear any conversations. Everett, Dawn, and Fault sat in a dark booth against the back wall.

Everett felt the pulse of the music and the chill of the alcohol move through him, and it seemed to him that he was nothing more than the sum of those effects.

"Do you remember my parents?" he asked Fault.

"I never met them," said Fault carefully. He seemed to sense Everett's darkness.

"Did I ever talk about them?"

"Not that I recall." Fault raised his beer glass and hid behind it.

"I thought I was coming back to something, if I came back here. To a self."

"When I found you in Vacaville, your name was Chaos. Remember *that?* Be grateful for what you have."

"Who you are isn't a matter of memories, anyway," said Dawn. "Especially lately."

"What is it, then?" Everett asked with bitter sarcasm. Only after it was out did he realize how badly he wanted an answer.

"It's what you do. Your choices." She sipped her drink. "Who you make yourself into."

"So I'm not supposed to care who I was before?"

Dawn shrugged. "Care if you want. Just don't make everything depend on it. Because you'll never be sure."

"What about you?" Everett said, suddenly furious at her smugness. "Why is it so easy for you? Do you remember everything before the break? Is your life now consistent with what it was then?"

"I'm mostly interested in forgetting what I was before," she said.

Everett weighed the notion of remembering too much, so much that you wanted to forget. He felt a flare of envy. Though it might not be that different, he supposed, from wanting not to dream. From drinking to blot out Kellogg.

"Were you married to Harriman, before?" he asked. "You're married, right?"

"Our alliance goes a long way back. It's not what you think, perhaps."

"What is he, some kind of dream scientist? What was he before?"

"His research was along those lines. The break changed it, like it did everything, of course. But I don't want to talk about Harriman. The subject bores me."

Everett slumped deeper in his seat, weary of pressing for answers that didn't satisfy. His gaze drifted out past the bar, through the front window, a pane cracked and repaired with masking tape and framed by dusty, obsolete logos.

There was someone he recognized on the street outside. Something, rather: the televangelist. It stood lecturing or reprimanding two small boys, who for a moment reminded Everett of Ray and Dave. But they weren't, of course. Just two boys. Everett watched as they ripped loose the televangelist's supply of pamphlets and scattered them on the avenue, then ran. The robot laboriously bent to gather the fluttering papers.

"Weren't you going to play some pool?" said Dawn unexpectedly to Fault.

Fault nodded, taking the hint, and slid out of the booth. Everett watched him approach the table, weaving his head nervously as he addressed the players.

"I want to talk to you about the girl in the dreams," Dawn said.

"What do you mean?"

"Gwen, right? You're in love with her. That's what you came back for."

Everett nodded, too tired and possibly too drunk to argue.

"Cale wants you to make his world real."

He looked away, not wanting to confirm it. He'd seen Dawn's contempt for Cale at the party.

"So he and the girl can be alive," she pressed on. "Don't lie, Billy told me all about it."

He met her eyes again and knew it was as good as nodding.

She scooted up against him in the booth, until shoulders, hips, and knees were all touching. "Listen," she said. "I have a better idea."

"Better than what?"

"Make me into Gwen."

"I don't understand."

"Use your power to turn me into the one you want. Then she'll be alive, and you'll have her. You can do it, you know. Make me into her, and we'll get away from here together. We can go to the house you dream about, if you want that."

He closed his eyes, then lifted his glass and drained it. He felt her hand on his thigh.

"That's somehow disgusting," he managed to say.

"Thank you," she said.

"Do you mind if I ask what's in it for you?"

She laughed and gripped his leg. "I could say that's none of your business, Everett. But I'll tell you. I would be young again—not that I'm old. But your Gwen is very young, like you. And I want my life to change. And you turn me on. Your power turns me on."

He didn't say anything.

"She would be real, Everett. I know how much you want that. You wouldn't have to wonder anymore."

"What about Harriman and Ilford? What about their plans?"

"I'd be happy to see their plans go up in smoke, dear." With the hand that had been on his knee she reached up and turned his face towards hers.

"Give me a kiss," she said.

He put his mouth on hers and tasted her breath. It was sweet, like apple juice. He'd somehow been expecting something bitter. Ash, or vinegar.

She turned her body towards his, and they moved together in the booth. Everett felt unstitched. The canned roar of the jukebox, the smell of sweat and stale smoke, the clack of billiard balls, Dawn's tongue in his mouth and her hand on his leg—all drifted apart like islands, to reveal the sea or fog that lay between.

He sat up and shook his head. Dawn opened her eyes, smiled petulantly, and drew away.

"You're not Gwen yet, you know," he said, wanting it to be a vicious remark, wanting it to express his entire cosmic bitterness.

But she was still smiling. "No. Not yet. But I'm not half bad."

He pushed out of the booth and made his way to the men's room, and stood, wobbling in place, at a stall. Fault came in after him, still carrying a pool cue.

"You all right, Everett?"

"Let's get out of here," said Everett.

He stood and looked up at the low sky, the vault of fog that pressed down on the black bracket of trees. Dawn had dropped them at the end of Ilford's driveway, and then her car had slipped invisibly into the night, the sound of the motor trailing away to silence.

For a moment he regretted letting her go. He could have gotten free of Ilford's looming house, could have followed Dawn to her bed and asked her questions. Her appeal was tied to what she seemed to know. He hated himself for the need that drew him to her. For his pastlessness.

He turned towards the house and encountered Fault, waiting for him. Suddenly he was filled with loathing. "You're the universal yes-man, aren't you?" he said.

"What?" said Fault, gaping through the darkness.

"You'll pimp me to anyone. Ilford, Cale, now Dawn—"

"That's a little harsh, Everett."

"Everyone wants a little piece of me," said Everett. "Except for you. For you I'm bait."

"There's a lot you don't understand," said Fault.

"Do you even care which side you're on?"

"I'm a survivor," said Fault indignantly. "Like you, like anybody else. I do what I have to do. You don't know about my problems, Everett. You don't know what happened to me."

There was silence then, as they stood in the dark on the drive. Everett heard his own breath, felt his own thick pulse swollen with alcohol. Before him glowed the windows of Ilford's living room, beacons in the fog. The basement apartment was unlit, invisible.

Finally he said, "You're right. I don't know what happened to you."

"That's right."

"So tell me. What happened to us in the break? What happened to Cale?"

"Things could be a lot worse."

"Who are you protecting? Ilford? Cale? Or yourself?"

"I'm not—"

"Tell me what you know, then."

"I can't." Fault turned away and walked towards the house.

Everett stood, infuriated, wanting to go the other way, into the fog and night. Instead he followed, moving into the circle of light that came from the windows. At the entrance to the basement he caught up with Fault again.

"I want a dose tonight," he said.

"Go upstairs and go to sleep. You're running through my supply."

"Give it to me, Billy."

"Shut up, don't talk about it out here—"

"Downstairs, then."

They went into the basement.

Y ou were away for so long," said Gwen.

"I've been busy," he said. "Things have been complicated."

She drew him to her, into her arms where she sat on the sketch of a bed in that empty space. He felt her touch like an echo, a whisper in the language of memory.

But he was tired of whispers.

"You have to find a way for us to be together," she said. "I can't stay here waiting for you anymore. I can't stand it."

"It's not that simple," he said.

"Cale said there was a way."

"Cale thinks there is a way. I don't know what I think."

"He said you could finish what he started," she said. "When he called me back, when he helped me come back. You could bring me into the world again."

Everett flinched. "Maybe. Maybe I could do something like that."

"Cale thinks so, Everett."

"Does Cale . . ." He stopped. It didn't matter if Cale came here. The thoughts she voiced were Cale's. It was better, in fact, to think that Cale came here, came to her in person and spoke. Better than thinking he'd somehow programmed her from afar. If it was that way, he didn't want to know.

He pulled away.

"Is something the matter?" She looked into his eyes.

"I need to know who I am."

"I know who you are."

"Tell me."

"You're Everett, in love with Gwen. Everett with Gwen. Just like I'm Gwen with Everett, Gwen for Everett." She blinked, looked down, then found his eyes again. "Do you love me, Everett?"

"Yes. But I'm not—"

"Then I know you."

"But you don't," he said. "You don't know me."

"What do you mean?"

He slid away from her on the bed. "Will you let me show you something?"

She nodded mutely.

He took her to Hatfork.

They stood in the parking lot of the Multiplex, the sun beating down on them, the desert air already drying their mouths. The theater's sign still shouted that Chaos was the only thing playing. The empty black lot burned them through the soles of their shoes. Squinting, he pulled her by the hand into the shelter of the entrance.

"Everett," she started.

"You have to call me Chaos," he said. He pulled out his old keys and unlocked the door to the staff entrance, and they stepped into the hall that led to the projection booth.

"Why should I call you Chaos?" She leaned back against the corridor wall, looking frightened.

"Because that's my name here." He reached out and touched her shoulder, and smiled slightly. "It might even be a name I gave myself. Because I'm part of why it's like this, here. I helped make this place."

"I don't understand. Places don't matter anymore. That's what Cale said. He said he could make any kind of place he wanted. And that you could too, Everett."

"This is different from the places Cale makes. I mean, I didn't make it by myself. I didn't even like it. But it's a part of me, it's the part of me I can remember."

He closed the door behind them, sealing them in the gloom. But he knew the way, would know the way forever. Grasping her hand, he led her up the stairs.

The projection booth was just as he'd left it, just as it always had been, the old machines layered in dust, his stained blankets balled underneath the couch. His cigarettes were where he'd left them, and he realized he hadn't had a smoke since hitting the road. He thought of that day, his argument with Kellogg out at the reservoir, his flight. He broke the spell of memory, led Gwen to a seat on the couch, and lit candles in the corners of the booth.

"This is what?" she said. "Where you lived?"

"For five years."

"I thought that was wrong, Everett. Cale told me you thought it was five years, but it wasn't really."

All she knew was what Cale told her. Everett saw that Cale had done his best to prepare her for her time with him, for her chance to be real.

"It doesn't matter," he said. "This is where I've been, this is what I remember. It was five years to me."

She shook her head, then stopped and stared at him, frowning. "You look different."

He nodded. His hair was a thatch here, his skin sunburnt, his teeth unbrushed.

She leaned back on the couch. "Okay," she said. "I've seen it. Now I know."

"No," he said. "You have to—you have to come with me. See it. I need you to see it all."

He took her in the car, and they drove through town. They went to Decal's first. Everett introduced Gwen, and Decal smiled his ragged grin and shook her hand. Decal gave them two quart containers of alcohol, which Chaos locked in the trunk. At Sister Earskin's he added a container of soup and two baked bird legs wrapped in recycled aluminum foil. Kellogg's Food Rangers still hadn't turned up any new cans. Chaos wondered how long it was since he'd seen a can or a Food Ranger, and a corner of him thought to wonder if the Rangers had actually existed in the first place or whether they were just another part of Kellogg's lore.

Then he drove them out to the edge of the desert, to sit by the crumbled salt dunes and watch the sunset and eat.

His thoughts were distant, and he and Gwen were silent for a long time. Finally, in the smallest voice she possessed, she said: "Did Cale make another place? A house for us? Like where you lived before?"

"Yes."

"Why don't we go there," she said, "instead of here?"

"I want you to see me here."

"Why?"

"You need to know this part of me."

"It's the worst part of you, Everett. You don't need this. You ran away from this."

"I—" He couldn't find the words.

"What?"

"Isn't that the idea, in love?" he said. "That you should be able to love the worst part?" But he knew this was beside the point, that he was talking about love when he should have been talking about real and fake.

"I don't know," she said.

"Well, I think that's all there is of me now, Gwen. The worst part. This part."

"I think you're being miserable," she said. The piece of bony meat she held, she placed it back on the foil. "And I think this food tastes rotten. I can't believe you had to make up all this garbage, make this whole screwed-up place, just to drag me here."

He stared off into the distance, at the sinking sun's reflection on the shimmering highway, and thought of his journey to California, the things he believed he was leaving behind, the things he believed he was moving towards.

"Cale says you can make anything," she said. "We can have whatever we want, Everett."

He didn't speak.

"Take us back," she said.

"Not yet."

She clung to his arm. "To your house, or whatever it is, then, please."

He turned and saw fear in her eyes. "All right," he said.

He put the food in the car and drove Gwen back to the Multiplex.

She sat on the couch, huddled into herself. "I'm scared, Everett. If you go away from me, I don't know what will happen. I don't know where I'll be. God, it smells in here."

"I don't want to go away from you," he said.

"Then stop this. It's destructive."

The sharpness in her voice was another echo of Cale.

"You've only been here a little while," he said. "Give it a chance."

"This is crazy, Everett—"

"Call me Chaos, please. It's important."

"No. I won't call you Chaos. It's not your name." She lowered her head and began crying quietly. "This is all wrong."

"Wrong?"

"I mean it's not you, not really. It's fake, Everett. It's not real. I wish I could make you understand."

"Everything is fake," he said. He opened a container of alcohol and took a drink. "It's all fake, now. But some fake things are important, too. Because they're the things that define a person. Like you, Gwen. You're one of the fake things that define me." He took another drink. "You're fake too, you know."

"Don't say that." The tears on her cheeks seemed to evaporate as her cheeks flushed with anger. "I came a long way back to you, Everett."

Cale's words. Every time she got angry, he heard Cale. Her gentle side was more convincing, because it had been cribbed from Chaos's dreams, but the angry parts had to be invented whole. And for that the only model Cale had was himself, the only voice he had was his own.

"Cale made you," he said at last, hating himself for saying it.

"No—"

"You're a simulation. He made you from a few scraps, a few memories. He built you around the idea of me, of us together. That's why that's all there is of you. He was counting on me to finish the job, to flesh you out and make you real."

"That's not what Cale told me."

"He lied to you. You're a slide show." He drank again, looking away, avoiding her eyes. "You're a gift for me, Gwen. Bait to bring me back. Cale did a good job, the best job he could. He made you believe in yourself."

She was crying again. "Can't you see it's me? Can't you hear my voice?"

"If you were really Gwen, you could love me here. As Chaos."

"I'm not obliged to love you at your worst," she said, standing up. "I'm not some dog, Everett."

He didn't speak, but thought, Nobody would bother to make a fake dog.

And the Hatfork part of him thought, If you were a dog, we'd have a roast. A major meal.

"This is all lies," she said and went to the door. "I don't have to pass some test. I'll see you later, Everett. I don't even *know* anyone named Chaos."

Groping for the wall of the stairwell in the dark, she closed the door behind her. He listened as her footsteps clattered away downstairs into silence.

Everett, who was little more than his tie to Gwen, might not have been willing to see her walk out. He might have followed her.

But Chaos didn't. Chaos reached for another drink.

As he drank, he wondered if the things he'd told her

were true, and what it would mean if they were. There was an ache inside him. He drank to blot it out. As he sat, he watched the candlelight blur, and the things he'd said and the things she'd said all echoed away like the unreal residue of one of Kellogg's dreams. What was left, what was always left, was this room. The old projectors pointing out on to the empty theaters.

What if what Cale suggested was actually true? Could he really dream projections into realities? Funny, if so. Because this sure wasn't what Cale had in mind. Hatfork.

He raised a drink to the thought.

He listened to the desert wind howling in the ventilation system. It was night now, outside. He wondered where the woman had gone, whether she'd made her way to the town, or the highway. Or had she disappeared the moment she left the building and went out of his range? Confusing. The whole business about San Francisco and the people there was confusing. Preposterous, really. Kellogg sure had some dumb ideas.

He remembered, sourly, the woman's parting words. Well, he wasn't so sure *he* knew anyone named Gwen, for that matter.

If Kellogg's ideas were dumb, what did that make him for dreaming them? Even dumber, he decided.

He stayed in his booth for two days, drinking, smoking, and masturbating. At night he drank to pass out, and didn't dream. It was hunger that finally flushed him. He got in the car and drove to Sister Earskin's for supplies. When he caught sight of himself in the rearview mirror, highway stretched out behind him, wind tangling his hair, he grinned. Everything was going to be okay. He could live with Kellogg's dreams. That was his job, his cross to bear. Hatfork was his place, after all; it was here that he was an emblem of something. Everything was back to normal.

Back at the Multiplex he found another car parked in the lot, one he didn't recognize. When he carried his bag upstairs, he found Kellogg waiting for him on the couch. Kellogg had the place lit with a beacon and was filling the air with smoke from a huge cigar.

"We gotta talk, Chaos."

Chaos couldn't find his voice. The last time they saw each other, he'd left Kellogg lying in the sand, bleeding.

"Your woman is staying at my place. And boy is she giving me an earful. She's even crazier than I am. Heh. You sure can pick 'em, Chaos."

"My woman?"

"Gwen. Your fancy-ass city woman, remember? How quickly, how quickly they forget. I should've named you Captain Vague. The Space Cowboy. Well, never mind. She and I are hitting it off just fine. Your loss, my gain. You dreamed yourself up a hell of a woman there, Captain."

Kellogg took a puff from his cigar, which glistened darkly. Chaos hallucinated briefly that it was studded with walnuts. That Kellogg was smoking a brownie.

"You and Gwen?" Chaos said. He remembered her now. Just.

Kellogg laughed, belching smoke. "A touch of jealousy, Captain?"

"What? No. She's not real."

"Not real? You're still riding that horse? You have got one profoundly fucked-up sense of priorities, Chaos. She's as real as I am. We both come from you."

"You're insane."

"Splendid!" said Kellogg, jumping up from the couch. Chaos took a step back. "Am I supposed to go 'No, *you're* insane'? We could do that for a while, I guess." He played both parts, crossing his eyes to perform Chaos: "You're in-

sane. No, you're insane. Excuse me, no, but you're insane."
He reached out and poked Chaos in the chest with the suck
end of the cigar, leaving a smear of tobacco-brown drool on
his tee shirt. "Give it up, Chaos. Sane and real only go so far
these days."

"Leave me alone."

Kellogg threw up his hands. "You're the boss. That's the
whole point, Chaos. You're in charge around here."

"Bullshit!" Chaos was suddenly roused. "I'm lost. I'm
in San Francisco, right?"

"Well, yeah . . ."

"And look. Here I am dealing with you again." Chaos
put his head in his hands. "I go all the way to San Francisco
and I can't even get away from you."

"What crap. You called *me* here, pal. I'm only a consul-
tant on this case."

Chaos ignored him. "I'm missing huge chunks of my
life," he went on. "I can't even remember my parents."

Kellogg waved his hand. "You're a thirty-year-old man,
Chaos. Time to stop whining about your parents. Start a
family of your own, for Chrissake."

"Who did this to me, Kellogg? Was it you?"

"Not me, pal. You were like this when I found you.
When you found me, when we started working together.
That's the way it has to be for you. You'll always be living in
an FSR."

"FSR?"

"Finite Subjective Reality. That's what I call it. I ought
to copyright that, in fact. You go creating a little area of control around you, until you bump into the next guy with his.
A little sphere of reality and unreality, sanity and insanity,
whatever you pull together. There's no hope of sorting it
out. That's the way you live. FSR."

"You have a theory for everything."

"True enough, true enough. And your FSR sure could use some sprucing up, Captain." Kellogg waved his hand and knocked over a candle. "Oops. Well, I must be going. Have a happy!" He picked up his beacon and started singing. "You take the high road, I'll take the low road, I'll be in Scotland before you . . ."

He stopped and turned. "Cripes, I almost forgot. Gwen wrote you a note." He dug in his pocket and pulled out a crumpled slip of paper. "Here you go."

He passed it to Chaos and clomped downstairs. Chaos smoothed out the note and read:

CALE CAN'T GET TO US HERE. YOU MADE IT SO HE CAN'T FIND US.
IF YOU DON'T DO SOMETHING WE'LL BE HERE FOREVER.

Chaos put the note on the table beside his cigarettes. He sat motionless for a minute or two, then unwrapped the food from Sister Earskin's and ate.

Late that night he was woken by quiet footsteps on the stairs. He sat up and lit a candle. The door opened and Melinda came in.

"You put me back with my parents, you dork."

He rubbed the sleep from his eyes and blinked at her.

Melinda flopped down on the end of the couch. "I ran away again, just now. They're gonna kill me."

"How did you get here?"

"I got Edge to drive me. He's got a crush on me, you know. Keeps trying to put a move on." She shook her head. "Can't believe I'm back in this town."

"Where's Edie?"

She sneered. "Now you want to know where Edie is. Boy, Chaos. You think maybe it's a little late?"

"What do you mean?"

"Back in Vacaville things are getting weird. Cooley and them . . ."

"What?"

"It's hard to explain. Anyway, where've you been? And what are we doing here?"

"I had to come back. I didn't mean to bring you. It has to do with this woman—"

"I know, I know. Your dream girl. Edge says she's up at Kellogg's. Why you want to drag her out here, though?"

"I had to see. I—my name isn't even Chaos, to her. I thought I was going back to my past. But there was nothing there."

"So?"

"It suddenly seemed important to be Chaos again."

"Well, maybe." Melinda rolled her eyes and yawned. "But I think you got the wrong Chaos."

"What do you mean?"

She tucked her legs up on the couch and rested her head on her knees. "You got the loser," she said. "The Chaos who just sat and took it. I mean, you could've picked the guy who hit the road."

He couldn't think of what to say.

"You know, because she might have fallen in love with *him*. If that's what you wanted, if you even know what you want." She yawned again. "God, I'm tired. I had to lie awake in the dark until my folks went to sleep. I was so pissed at you. Oh." She woke up a bit. "You lose a clock? I found one outside."

Then she went to sleep, curled up there at his feet. As though she thought it was her right place, he mused. Whatever she had against him.

He sat for a long time watching her sleep. When he was sure it wouldn't wake her, he slipped out and went downstairs. The sun was just beginning to rise. He turned and saw the last visible stars at the edge of the hills to the west.

He found the clock lying on a small bank of gravel at the far end of the parking lot. It was surprisingly heavy, and the golden pendulum shifted erratically as he righted it. Strangely, the loud tick was regular whether the clock was upright or not. He stared at it wonderingly. There was nothing in Hatfork or Little America so clean and beautiful.

Another message, another arrow pointing him away from Hatfork. But an odd, unexpected one.

He had to return, he saw now. There was something unfinished in the place the clock was from. Maybe an escape he hadn't managed yet. The tick of the clock seemed to drown out clear thought, even as it called him back.

Chaos walked out to the sign at the end of the parking lot and from there watched the sun rise over the desert, watched as it warmed the hills and burned away the dew that clung to the grass that grew in the cracks in the pavement and around the foot of the sign.

C H a O s, c H A O s, C h A o S.

Then he let Hatfork disappear; the sky, the desert, the Multiplex, and the girl sleeping upstairs; everything.

Τhe clock was happy.

It felt itself to be the very embodiment of pride and purpose, clacking. The work was second nature, effortless. To be a clock was to tick, but to be *this* clock was to clack. The sound itself was golden. And reflection; that was the great work, the distinction.

The curved casing of the clock held the whole room in miniature, bent and gilded. But the light flowed both ways. As the shimmering pendulum swung again and again, an inch from the glass table, magical specks of light raced along the walls of the room, touching everything, dancing in flamboyant courses that were repeated exactly. The beams confirmed the arrangement of the room, each item glowing in its right place, even as the reflection in the casing drew all together into a detailed, burnished knot.

Conferred, conferring. What a privilege.

Clack.

The room was happy all over. The clock was aware of the fantastic pleasure the oak chair took in just being the oak chair, claiming nothing more. It was possible even to envy the oak chair, grain glowing beneath so many fine thin layers of varnish, wooden spokes of the seat back marvelously warped. Ilford might sit there! But then the clock knew that when Ilford entered the room through any doorway and stood or sat anywhere, he would be held and honored in the clock's gleaming case, would experience the clock's counting as a steadying pulse, and that was better.

The chair was fine, but the clock was finer.

The clock felt the satisfied presences of all the furnishings in the room, the paintings, the glass table, the lamp with the marble base, even the row of beveled glasses and the stoppered crystal bottle of scotch behind the doors in the inlaid-rosewood cabinet. Even the bonsai trees in a row on the mantel—except for that one at the end, which seemed a little edgy, a little discontented.

Clack, clack.

Today it was raining through the fog, so the windows were jeweled with reflective drops themselves. They twinkled. The fog kept the windows opaque, not so much portals to the outside as mirrors of the room, even when it wasn't raining. The clock faced no competition from the sun. All light and warmth emanated from the room, and the clock was the shining center of that system. Nothing else was as sure. The clock had never been fogged over. The sun almost always was.

The room was perfect but incomplete. Unavoidably, it was waiting, a little unfulfilled, for Ilford to return. What was the point of the perfection, the soft glowing, if not for Ilford to move through and inhabit? This wasn't just any perfect room—as if there were any other—it was Ilford's perfect room.

Clack.

The clock and the rest of the room didn't have to wait long today. Ilford came in, alone, shaking rain from his coat onto the carpet. Taken strictly, his presence created imperfection, the droplets soaking into the weave, the cabinet door now ajar as he poured himself a drink, the clinking and clunking of his movements, so disorderly beside the metronomic voice of the clock. As groomed and clean as Ilford was, he was no match for his own house. But that didn't matter. With him inside, the house could really live and breathe, fulfilled.

The clock, for one, admired Ilford enormously. It couldn't completely say why; in fact, it couldn't begin to. But reflecting Ilford so that he was unified in golden miniature with his perfect possessions, upholding the standard of Ilford's perfect reasonableness and good judgment with unerring timekeeping, these duties—privileges, really—were the point of the clock's whole being—

Then something was wrong.

Clack.

Instead of moving unself-consciously past the clock, moving with his usual ease, his body speaking with every gesture that he possessed his perfect house with that indifferent, casual power that thrilled the clock and thrilled all the furnishings, Ilford had stared. As he set his glass of scotch on the glass table, he had turned his head a little awkwardly and stared with wide-eyed uncertainty right at the clock's face, and his hand had trembled, just a little.

This passed, but was replaced by something else inappropriate, something obscene. Ilford's insecure look switched to one that was possessive and gloating. He looked at the clock as though it were something threatening that had been subdued, a lion's head stuffed and mounted on a hunter's wall, instead of the devoted and faithful servant that it was.

Neither look should have been necessary.

Clack.

The clock became troubled. Ilford raised his glass and drank, and everything was normal again. The clock knew that none of the other furnishings had noticed, that they were all sure of their place around Ilford, and Ilford's place among them, presiding. Only the clock was disturbed.

It had seen the two odd looks, and something else. In Ilford's features, as he moved through the disconcerting sequence, the clock had also seen a flicker, an erasure, of some other face. The clock might have credited that flicker to *youthfulness* if it hadn't been for the doubts already forming.

As it was, the clock groped for a description of the wrongness etched in the margins of Ilford's features. And when it groped, it found an answer. Cale.

Who was Cale?

As the clock began to remember, it became very frightened. It went on keeping perfect time, even as it began to remember that just as Ilford was not only Ilford but also the subsumed presence, so the clock was not only a clock. In fact, the part of the clock that mattered wasn't a clock at all.

Clack.

Ilford lifted his drink and rose from the couch, his posture perfect, command completely restored. Outside, the rain fell, but Ilford didn't pause to glance at the windows. He moved towards the stairs to the second floor. The room was mildly disappointed to see him go, but it honored the decision, even offered silent murmurs of encouragement and congratulations.

The room didn't object, but the clock did. The clock suddenly didn't want Ilford out of its sight.

So it stopped time. Ilford stood frozen where he stood, one foot lifted to the bottom step, the scotch in his glass tilted against gravity in the same direction as the stopped pendulum of the clock.

"I'm leaving," the clock told the bonsai at the left-hand end of the mantel.

"Ilford won't let you," said the potted tree bluntly. "Look at what he's done already to keep you here."

"He's a dreamer, isn't he?"

"I didn't think I had to tell you," said the bonsai. "But I never can figure out how much other people understand."

"Billy," said the clock, "I want you to tell me what Ilford did with Cale."

"I can't," said the tree, shaking.

"Why not?"

"Ilford would kill me if I told. Just like he'll kill me if you go."

"He turned you into a part of his living room, Billy," said the clock.

"Maybe this is just temporary," said the bonsai hopefully. "He sort of panicked when you disappeared yesterday. Where did you go?"

"Back to Hatfork. Or a version of Hatfork, anyway. I was there for a couple of days." The clock suddenly wondered what happened in Wyoming—had time stopped for them too while Everett borrowed their reality?

"Is that where you're going now?" The bonsai sounded frightened.

"I don't think so. But I'm leaving here. So you might as well tell me what you know."

"Ilford will do anything to keep you here."

"Why does he need me, if he's a dreamer? Why can't he do it himself?"

"You're different. Your talent is completely *plastic,* that's his word for it. You're suggestible."

"How is that different?"

"His dreams only work like wish fulfillment. He moves people around, rearranges things so they suit him better."

"Is that what happened to Cale and Gwen?"

"To lots of people," said the bonsai defensively. "Like Dawn. You remember Dawn from before?"

"No."

"Dawn is Cale's mother. She used to be Ilford's wife, Dawn Hotchkiss. But then he was angry at her, and Harriman liked her, so—"

"Then where did Cale go? And Gwen?"

"It's worse for some people," said the bonsai quietly.

"Worse how?"

"Ilford turns people—into things. That's why he has so many things."

The clock considered the living room, the furnishings all arrayed in perfect splendor. The glowing, emanating furniture. And the kitchen loaded with improbable supplies.

There might be things worse than being a clock, the clock realized.

Ilford still stood rigidly in place, poised just before the stairs in defiance of gravity and momentum. The clock held the pendulum to one side, fighting time's progression. It was an effort, like talking with one's breath held.

Outside, the rain was frozen on the windows in mid-twinkle. There was the silence of a roar hushed.

The bonsai had begun crying, its leaves trembling help-lessly, its voice reduced to a sniffling squeak.

"Why do I have to be the only one who remembers?" it said finally.

The clock was silent for a long time. "I don't know," it said.

"I only brought you back because I thought you could help Cale," said the tree. "I don't care about Ilford's plans. I was just holding on for Cale. But you probably don't even care. You can't remember Cale, so it doesn't matter to you."

"I remember a little. When I saw the tape—"

"The tape is nothing," said the bonsai angrily. "I re-member before. When Cale was real."

"But he's still here," said the clock. "In your fridge."

"Cale was strong. When everything changed, when Il-ford made everything change, he survived. He was working on virtual reality stuff on his computer, and he was still alive in there, hiding in the computer. That's where all the world-building stuff comes from. Then Ilford destroyed the com-puter."

"What about the drugs?"

The bonsai hesitated. "I guess that comes from my inter-ests at the time," it said awkwardly.

Computers and drugs. The clock recalled the first dream Chaos had on the road after getting out of Kellogg's range. The dream of the house by the lake. His interests there had been pretty much along the same lines.

"So Cale hid there," said the clock. "In your refriger-ator."

"It wasn't something Ilford thought he had to take away

from me. He always left me pretty much alone. I guess that's because I was so supremely fucking harmless."

"But Cale's in Ilford, too."

"That's not Cale," said the bonsai with fury. "Just a piece of him that Ilford stole."

"What about Gwen?"

"Gwen wasn't as strong as Cale."

The clock thought for a minute and decided it didn't want to know any more about that.

"What happened to me?" it asked. "How did I end up in Wyoming?"

"You were here just after the change. You don't remember?"

The clock, wanting to shake its head, almost let the pendulum swing free. "No," it said instead.

"He wanted you to work with him. He and Cale were fighting about it all the time. Then you and Gwen were going to leave. That's when everything happened." The bonsai started crying again. "Even Cale doesn't remember, only me."

"You mean, that's when Ilford changed everything."

The tree made a confirming sound.

"How did I get away?"

"You dreamed something that made us all crazy," sniffled the tree. "When we came out of it, you were gone, to Wyoming, I guess. Making weird scenes in the desert."

It made sense, the clock thought. Everett ran until he got to Little America, where he found someone who could cancel his dreaming. Kellogg.

And Kellogg had helped Everett finish the job Ilford started. Of making him forget his life.

"You just stayed," said the clock. "You never ran."

211

"Yes," said the tree.

"You're pretty devoted to Cale."

"I thought if Ilford got what he wanted, maybe Cale could come back. And then I thought you could bring him back."

"I can't."

"Why not?"

"I just can't. Even if I could, it would be like Gwen, the way Cale brought Gwen back."

"Then you might as well go," said the bonsai, sounding defeated. "If you can," it added.

The clock considered Ilford stuck in midstep, the rain and fog stilled where it clung outside the house. It remained difficult to believe in a world outside this room, in entities that were other than furnishings, in a human other than Ilford.

The clock hated Ilford. Hated the room Ilford had devised, hated being the clock. Hated those things so fiercely that it dreamed awake, a crude dream of fury.

And the floor fell away beneath them.

Like an explosion, they landed in the basement—Everett, Fault, and Ilford raining down into Cale's apartment with the chairs, lamps, cabinets, paintings, plants, and the glass coffee table, which shattered across the worn couch in the middle of the basement floor. Fault landed in a pile of wrecked bonsai: dirt and ceramic shards laced with ancient roots. The golden clock smashed against the concrete at Everett's head, and clacked just once as it expired, as if to post last notice that time had resumed before dying in the line of duty. Ilford was still clutching his glass of scotch when he collided with the top of the battered refrigerator. The glass was dashed to pieces from the impact, and Ilford slid to the floor, his hand gashed and bleeding, his shirt soaked with scotch.

Everett looked back up at the living room. The floor had disappeared, uniting Ilford's home with Fault's hovel. And the walls had been sucked clean, the contents drawn down by some cataclysmic force; even the marble mantelpiece now rested, cracked, against the basement door. A painting of Ilford gazing majestically into the fogged bay had been impaled on Fault's lamp.

Outside, the rain fell steadily, brushing through the leaves of the trees, tapping at the cobblestones.

Ilford and Fault both pulled themselves out of the wreckage and stood checking themselves, dabbing at cuts, shaking their heads.

Everett didn't bother checking himself. "Get out of here, Billy," he said.

"What do you mean?" said Fault.

"Go. Run away."

"Where?"

Ilford stood staring groggily.

"Don't you have anyone to go to?" asked Everett.

"I had Cale."

"Go south and join Vance's army, then. They'll see you and pick you up. Just go, Billy. But give me the bike key first."

"What?"

"The ignition key. I need it."

"When you say run, you're not kidding," said Fault.

Everett took the key. Fault stepped over the cracked mantel and went out into the rain. He looked back once, and Everett waved him on. Fault picked his way through the garden, then broke into a run and disappeared beyond the foggy treeline at the neighboring yard.

"I'm leaving now, Ilford," said Everett.

Ilford held his right hand over the gash on his left. His face had become a site of violence, a battlefield. The older man he should have been was evident now, and at war with what he'd stolen from time and from Cale.

"You destroyed my house," he said.

"I'm glad," said Everett.

"We'll catch you," said Ilford. "The first time you fall asleep you'll dream, and we'll find you and bring you back."

"You should hope I never fall asleep again," said Everett. "I've got a plan for you. I've got a dream in mind."

"You can't control what you dream."

"I've been practicing," said Everett. "When I went away to Hatfork just now, weeks passed for me. I spent a long time refining my talent."

It was a bluff, but Everett knew it was good enough. He knew he was in charge now.

"You know I can't let you go," said Ilford. He moved to a spot between Everett and the door, picking his way over the shattered remains of his living room. "There are things to be accomplished here." The words were a pathetic echo of his and Harriman Crash's rhetoric.

"It's over," said Everett. "I know what you did."

"What I did," Ilford repeated stiffly.

"Fault told me."

"Told you what?"

"Get out of my way," Everett said.

"All you know how to do is run," said Ilford. "We're the same, except I stay and try to build. You just run."

"If I did what you did, I'd run too. Maybe running is a good thing when you're like this."

"You can't run forever."

"Well, I'd rather try. Than turn into you." Everett suddenly saw his running as a talent, one more distinctive than the dreaming, even. It was what he'd had to offer Melinda back in Hatfork. It would be what he offered Edie now.

"You can't stop me from leaving," said Everett. "I'm stronger than you. I stopped your clock."

"You don't care about Cale," said Ilford. "You're leaving him behind."

"Cale is dead, Ilford. You killed him."

Ilford looked over at the refrigerator. "I know about the drug, Everett. You think Billy could keep that from me? You think I don't know what's happening right below my feet?"

Everett didn't speak.

"I'll really kill him if you leave."

Everett went to the refrigerator. The lock still hung loose where he'd pried it apart the day before. He opened it and took out the rack of vials.

He took one and put it in his pocket. Then lifted the rack and hurled it at Ilford's feet. It smashed into a mass of glass shards and ooze, drugs mixing with the soil from the bonsai trees and with the tangled clock innards.

Ilford looked down dispassionately at the mess.

"That's not what I meant," he said. "That's *Billy's* Cale you just destroyed. Billy prefers the drug version because he can't face what really happened. It's easier to blame it all on me, to think I simply wiped Cale away."

"What are you talking about?"

"What really happened, Everett. Cale got sick. It wasn't my fault."

"Sick?"

"Look."

Everett turned. At the long window on the far side of

the basement, seated facing the rain, was a figure in a wheelchair, a withered, defeated body, back curved around a wasted chest, wrists sagging against the arms of the chair. The figure's head was tilted slightly, away from the window, towards Everett, and though it was mostly in darkness, a hint of familiar features was visible in the soft light that glistened through the window.

It was Cale. Not the Cale from the tape or the Cale in the drug or the Cale that flickered in Ilford's face. A realer, sadder Cale.

Everett felt his certainty leaking away like the water trickling through the gaps in the cobblestone. Felt his departure and his fury plucked from him and replaced with weariness and doubt. He would have to stay.

He moved towards the figure, his foot catching on the broken pendulum.

"Don't," said Ilford. "He's very vulnerable to infection, he can't be touched—"

As Everett plodded through the wreckage towards the dim figure, something happened, something changed.

"Not so close," said Ilford, his voice rising with panic.

The wheelchair was heaped with meat in a rough approximation of a human form. The frozen roasts, lamb shanks, and slabs of beef from the gigantic freezer upstairs.

Not Cale.

Everett pushed the wheelchair, and the chunks of meat cascaded down, to roll in the dust and debris on the floor. The biggest piece, a glistening rack of ribs, settled into the seat of the chair, leaving a smear of grease and frost on its leather back.

It was just another trap, Everett thought. Another thing Ilford had set up while Everett was dreaming himself in Hatfork. A backup in case the clock didn't hold him.

Or possibly it was something more, something awful. Everett turned to Ilford.

"You should have stayed where I am," said the old man bitterly. "He looked okay from a distance. When the light is right, you can see him coming back."

"You only dream people into things," said Everett. "You can't reverse it."

Ilford was distinctly smaller and older now. His voice was almost lost in the sound of the rain.

"I'm trying," he said. "I keep trying."

"You said you'd kill him," said Everett. "But he's not even here. There's no one to kill. And there's nothing keeping me here."

"I'd never kill my own son," said Ilford, his voice finally breaking, turning inward. "How could you think I'd do that?"

Everett went past him to the door, pausing only to check that the motorcycle keys were safe in his pocket.

He led the televangelist out of the rain, into the shelter of an abandoned storefront on a sidestreet off Submission. The onscreen face looked bewildered.

"I have something for you," he said, and took out the vial from Fault's refrigerator.

The video face stared. "What is it?"

"What you've been looking for, I think. God." He pressed it into the televangelist's ferroplastic palm. "Be careful with it. Store in a cool, dry place."

"What kind of God is it?" asked the robot.

"The world-making kind," Everett said. "The kind you're missing. It knows about wanting to be real instead of programmed, things you want to know. This is the first time it's been available in this form."

The face frowned. "The first time?"

"Yes. There's a lot of bogus God going around. But this is the real thing."

"How can I—access this God?"

"A problem," he admitted. "You and your friends will have to figure that out. You have to take it in somehow. Let it alter your program."

He looked at the televised face and imagined Cale there instead. Like the face from the videotape he'd watched in Vacaville. Full circle. Only now Edie would be right. Cale would exist only on television.

He wondered if the robots would go up the hill and kill Ilford, when Cale got inside them.

"Thank you," said the televangelist.

"You're welcome."

The robot strode purposefully into the rain. Everett watched it walk away, then he went back to the motorcycle.

Ten minutes later he crossed the hump of the bridge over the bay, and the tall buildings dropped out of sight behind him. In the Oakland hills he rode out of the rain. The highway was empty, and he didn't have to stop until the bike ran out of gas a few miles short of Vacaville.

He junked it and, for the second time, walked in.

Things were different. He noticed that from the first. Nobody he passed on the street seemed right. As in the mirror room of a funhouse, everyone was taller or shorter or wider than they should be, or else they were missing a limb or two. He saw an albino and a dwarf and a man with a foot-long nose, but he didn't see anyone he recognized. Nobody was proportioned right. It gave him a headache. And they all slinked along the sidewalks like they barely had a right to be there, avoiding one another's eyes, and his.

It was nearly sundown. He found his way downtown, where he made an immensely fat woman on a park bench look up from the comic book she was reading—it featured svelte, well-proportioned government stars—and give him directions to the luck-testing offices. She blinked out at him through her mask of flesh and pointed the way.

He found Cooley's office, but Cooley wasn't there. His secretary was a woman with a set of complicated braces supporting spindly, withered legs. She looked at him suspiciously, but when he gave the name Chaos, her eyes widened.

"I need to know where Edie Bitter moved," he said. "Where she's living now."

"Mr. Cooley needs to talk to you," she said. "He'll want to know you're here."

"I'll talk to Ian later. He'll be able to find me."

"Excuse me," she said. "Please wait outside."

He went out into the hallway, to be stared at by a shrunken man who sat waiting perched on the edge of a bench. Everett nodded, and the man nodded back, smiling.

"You're pretty, but I'm not in love with you," said the man.

"What?" said Everett.

"You're pretty, but I'm not in love with you. I don't even know you. Why's that?"

"I don't know what you're talking about."

"You must be here because they're going to make you famous now. Is that right?"

"No."

"Don't be modest. I probably ought to get your autograph. You'll be on TV. The girls will love you. We'll all love you."

"No, really."

"Then you must be in trouble. It's got to be against the law to be so good-looking if you're not one of them."

The conversation was interrupted by the clatter of the secretary appearing on her ungainly, stiltlike braces. She glared at Everett and the dwarf angrily.

"Here." She handed Everett a slip of paper. "I called Mr. Cooley. You can go now. That's the address. He says he'll see you tomorrow. After you get adjusted."

"Adjusted?"

She frowned. "Look, I don't know who you think you are, Mr. Chaos. But you're showing very little respect for— the way we do things around here."

"I've been away."

"I can see that."

"I've got questions—"

"Save them for Ian. Please go." She turned and hobbled back into the office.

He walked to the eastern edge of town, the windows ahead reflecting flashes of the low orange sun behind him. The streets he passed were increasingly residential and quiet. He found the address on the note, a two-story apartment building, the upper floor cantilevered out over a parking space. Edie's station wagon was in the lot.

The woman who came to the door presented a problem. She was Edie, but she also wasn't. She was about four feet tall, taller than the man at Cooley's office but not by much. Her body wasn't disproportionate, though. A midget, he thought, not a dwarf, remembering the distinction.

She had Edie's features drawn in precise miniature on her face.

"Chaos?" she said, her voice high but recognizable.

"Yes," he said, and then didn't know what else to say.

"Do you want to come in?" she said.

He nodded and followed her inside.

The scene there was a bizarre analogue of the one he'd left: two boys watching television. But Ray was enormously fat. As wide as he was tall, he took up half the couch. Dave sat on one of the arms. At first Everett assumed he was just making room for his brother. Then he spotted Dave's tail, protruding through a gap in the back of his pants and hanging down the side of the couch.

Melinda came out of the bedroom. She hadn't changed. She looked from Everett to Edie to Everett, then ran up and threw her arms around him.

"I didn't know where you were," she said, her face pressed against his side.

"It took longer than I thought." He met Edie's eyes as he said this.

Melinda backed away. "I saw you in Hatfork. You remember that?"

"Yes," he said, surprised.

"Thought I was going crazy."

Edie left, walking on her tiny legs into the kitchen. Ray and Dave just sat and stared at Everett, the television blaring behind them.

"Melinda," said Everett. "Would you take Ray and Dave outside? The sun's nice."

She made a wry face, but turned and said with exaggerated weariness, "C'mon, guys." She waved her hand, and Ray and Dave hurried after her, Ray wobbling like jello.

He went into the kitchen. Edie, characteristically, had busied herself washing dishes. But now she had to stand on a chair to do it.

He wanted to rush to her, embrace her unhesitatingly, the way Melinda had embraced him, but it seemed clumsy, impossible. Would he lift her like a child? He wanted her to be as she was before, and at the same time he wanted, desperately, to make her know this didn't matter. The two impulses fought in him, one shaming the other.

She finally turned, her eyes full of fear and confusion.

"What happened, Edie?"

"You went away," she said with sudden bitterness.

"I'm sorry about that," he said, very softly. "I wish I hadn't. But what happened here?"

"Nothing," she said defensively. She pulled off the rubber gloves and sat down on the chair. "We moved a few times, of course. I'm working in a cardboard recycling factory this week. Melinda had her luck tested—did she tell you? No, of course not. Well, it was very good, Ian was very impressed . . ."

"What about—what happened to this place? To Ray and Dave?" He avoided saying: You're a midget.

"What's wrong with Ray and Dave?" she said angrily.

"Forget it. Just come sit with me on the couch."

They went back to the living room and sat. He still couldn't bring himself to touch her, didn't feel he knew how. Yet it was what he was here for, what he wanted most.

"Did you come to take Melinda away?" said Edie. "Is that what this is all about? You know I can't stop you. It's not my choice. But that girl needs—"

He held up a hand. "Edie, listen. I came back because of you. Not Melinda. I mean, Melinda too, both of you together. I want to live with you. Here or away from here. If it's okay."

"What are you saying?"

"I love you, Edie."

"Please don't," she said quickly.

"What?"

"I don't need talk like that. It doesn't make sense. I know who you love. You're just like everyone else. You love the girl on the television."

"No—"

"Yes. I saw her, before. In your dreams, over and over. And then on television, when you got that tape."

"That was a mistake, Edie."

"No." She shook her head and smiled sadly. "Don't feel bad. That's how it is. The people on television are better. You don't have to be ashamed. Did you find her?"

"Sort of. It wasn't right."

"You shouldn't say that. It's a very lucky thing if someone famous—from the government or television—cares about you. That's a very special thing. I have that, it's the only kind of luck I have."

Everett felt a blur of confusion. Did she mean Cooley?

"Edie," he said, and then he leaned over and put his lips to hers, felt her tiny nose against his, felt her eyelashes brush his cheek. At first her mouth was still, and all he felt was a trace of startled breath against his lips. Then she closed her eyes and kissed him, the force of all her passion behind it for a tantalizing moment. Just as quickly, she drew back.

"Oh, Jesus," she sighed.

"Edie, it's me. Please say you remember—"

"I remember, Chaos, but this isn't right. You went away, and I understood. You could never love me." She pointed to herself. "I don't understand why Ian does."

"You weren't like this," he blurted out. "You're a beautiful woman. Something they did changed it, made everybody here look different."

"That's silly," she said, nervously. "This is me. Please, Chaos, go away now. Don't torture me. Love the girl on television. She's the one who's beautiful."

"I want you," he said. "You were beautiful. You still are. Lots of people are beautiful, not just the ones on television."

"Ordinary people are ugly. Look around, Chaos." She looked away.

"I remember," he said. "You were like a woman in a magazine. You loved showing your body to me."

"You're being hateful. Why can't you face the truth? I'm ugly, Chaos." She choked back tears.

"Something happened here, the dreamers in charge of Vacaville, they went overboard. They want you to think they're the only—"

"Shut up!" Her tiny voice was ragged with fury. "This is my life! I live here! I don't need you coming here and telling me about how you think it ought to be. You came here once and I listened to you, and you screwed everything up and then you left. Don't do this to me again! If you want to stay, then go get your luck tested. Maybe you belong on television, Chaos. Maybe you're special. But I'm not! Leave me alone!"

"This is crazy." He wanted to pick up where he'd left off, wanted reality to sit still for him for once. "There aren't just fifteen or twenty attractive human beings in the world. I mean, if you aren't special, then what does Ian want with you, anyway?"

"That's private," she hissed.

Agitated with jealousy, he jumped up from the couch. He needed room to think. "Where are the keys to your car?"

"Where are you going?"

"I want to prove it to you. How late is the mall open?"

"I don't know. I mean, it's still open . . ."

"Here, then." He held out his hand, and she passed him the keys. "I'll be back."

"Chaos." Her voice was small, her anger replaced by confusion. "I don't like this."

"Well, you can write me a ticket, a summons, when I get back."

He went outside and found Melinda, and without explaining dragged her away from Ray and Dave and into Edie's car.

"Tell me what's going on here," he said.

"Hey, I *told* you things were getting weird."

He started the car, pulled out into the street. "So you remember talking to me in Hatfork?"

"Yup. Saw my folks, and that guy Edge. Saw the messed-up place you live in, too. How'd you do that?"

He shook his head. "Forget it. Listen, doesn't anybody here remember two weeks ago?"

"Yeah, sure. They remember it *wrong*. Everybody started changing, and I tried to say something to Edie, but it was like they thought they were always like that. They just started watching TV even *harder*."

"Changing? Getting ugly, you mean?"

"Yup. Except for Cooley and his pals. They got everyone looking awful so they could look good. Only they left me alone." She laughed. "Guess they thought I was strange enough to look at like I was."

"And it worked, didn't it? Edie's sleeping with Cooley now." He had to know.

"Yup. But it's not her fault."

He kept his eyes on the road.

"That's what it's like here now," Melinda said. "Everybody's in love with the government. She can't help it. He's been hittin' on her for a long time, too."

He turned and saw she was squinting at him. "What?" he said.

"You look funny," she said. "You gain some weight?"

"Funny?"

"It's nothing," she said, too quickly. "You probably just been eating good, after all those cans. I been doing the same thing." She lifted her shirt and ruffled the margin of fur at her waist. "Where'd you go, anyway?"

"I saw some old friends. I'll tell you about it later." He parked the car in the mall lot. "Wait here."

He hurried through the mall, to the shop he'd seen before, where they sold comic books and magazines. He wanted to buy a copy of *Playboy* or *Penthouse*, to show Edie that beautiful bodies were everywhere, that the Vacaville cabal didn't have the market cornered.

He found the shop, but the rack with the adult magazines was missing.

He asked the clerk, a normally proportioned man whose appearance was ruined by a raspberry birthmark that covered his face like a splayed-out octopus. "We keep those behind the counter now," the clerk explained. "What'll it be —endomorph?"

"What?"

"You know the new law, right?"

"New law? I just want to buy a copy of *Playboy*."

"Fine. But the new law says you get the issue that corresponds to your body type. Midgets look at midgets, and so on." He swept his arm back, indicating the rack behind the cabinet. Sure enough, there were ten or twelve different versions of *Playboy*, and the bodies Everett glimpsed on the covers were all distorted and wrong.

The clerk gave him the once-over. "Looks like endomorph to me," he said. He flopped a magazine onto the counter. The woman on the cover was leering and enormous.

"What are you talking about?"

"Take a look, fella."

Everett caught sight of himself in the window of the shop. He was hideously soft and fat, his cheeks jowly, his hands like tufts of dough.

"That'll be four dollars," said the clerk.

"That's not what I want," he said, a hopeless feeling settling over him. "I need to show someone something. I need a picture of a *nice* body. The way *Playboy* used to be."

"They still make it like that," nodded the clerk. "But only government stars can buy it."

"Can't you sell me one? Nobody will know. It's important."

"Hey, fella, you think you're the only one wants the good stuff? Cripes. I can't sell it to you, can't even look at it myself, and believe you me, I would. But they keep it locked up. Only the government stars have the keys."

"You expect me to believe the customers have the keys and you don't?"

The clerk looked rueful. "Well, they don't actually pay, you know. In fact, we pay them to come and get it from us. Supposed to add prestige to the establishment."

"Shit."

"But if you want to look at them, you can," said the clerk helpfully. "They just got their clothes on." He indicated *People*, *Rolling Stone*, and *TV Guide*. The cover of *Rolling*

Stone showed Palmer O'Brien, and *People* featured President Kentman with his arm around Ian Cooley. "They're nicer to look at than this stuff anyway," said the clerk confidentially.

"I don't want to look at *them*," said Everett. "I want to look at *other* people who look nice."

"But that's all the good *Playboy* is anyhow." The clerk sounded confused. "Pictures of them without their clothes. Why would they want to look at anyone but themselves?"

"Forget it," said Everett. He stalked out, or tried to, but his increasingly heavy body made sudden movement impossible. Everything was buffered in layers of flesh. So he oozed out instead and slammed the door behind him.

Moving back through the mall, he found that now he fit in. The people he passed weren't made uncomfortable by his presence anymore. He belonged. Soon maybe he'd be in love with a government star too.

He squeezed into the car, but it was work, and he had to move the seat back. Melinda looked him up and down and said, "You're definitely putting on weight."

"We have to get out of here."

"I was waiting for you to say that. Try telling Edie, though."

He started the car, marveling at the flesh of his fingers, how far the key and steering wheel seemed from the bones of his hand.

"Don't tell me you're leaving her here, you crumb."

"No," he said. "We'll take her."

"And Ray and Dave, right?"

He nodded.

By the time they got back, night had fallen. Ray and Dave were in front of the television. Edie was there too. They all looked up and watched as he rumbled into the apartment, but nobody said anything.

He slumped, defeated, into an armchair. Edie went quietly into the kitchen and came back with a beer for him, and he drank it and stewed in his thoughts while the others all watched television.

He waited for the evening to end, for the boys to be put to bed. It seemed to take forever. No one spoke. They crept around him in his chair like an obstacle. It made him think of Vance's description of the tumors that grew inside the houses in Los Angeles.

Finally Ray and Dave were asleep, and Melinda was in her room. Edie nodded to him, still not breaking the silence, and indicated the bedroom. He followed her inside, and she closed the door. She climbed up on the bed and sat on one of the pillows.

"Here." She patted the pillow beside her with a tiny hand. "Will you come sit down?"

He went and sprawled on the bed glumly, keeping his distance. For their bodies to touch now would be even more absurd. But apparently she didn't think so, because she reached for his hand. However disparate their sizes, at least he was her equal now in ugliness. But he would have to get over all that, it seemed. Caring about size and ugliness.

"I'm sorry I freaked out, Chaos. It was a shock to have you come back."

"It's okay. I just . . . I don't know what to do. I came here because of you."

"That's okay," she said softly.

"But everything seems screwed up. I don't think I can stay here, in Vacaville. I want to take you somewhere else."

"Where?" She looked frightened again.

"I don't know. But this is no good."

"You always talk like that, and I never know what you mean."

"Edie," he started, then stopped and began again. "Edie, you would understand if you went away. The way it is here, the way they have it, you can't think clearly about things. But you'd understand if you got out. Will you trust me?"

She nodded.

"Do you—want to be with me? I mean, instead of with Ian?"

"Yes," she said.

"You're sure?"

"I'm sure. I don't want to be with Ian." He felt her hand trembling in his.

"What?"

"There's something I didn't tell you. When I'm with Ian . . . I don't know how he does this, but my body changes. I'm not small anymore. I'm different, beautiful. Only while we're . . . together. Do you understand?"

"Yes."

A tear crossed her cheek. "I don't understand what it is. But it made me—want to do it. To experience that. I hated him, but at the same time—"

"You don't have to explain."

She sniffled.

"Going away will mean that Ray and Dave won't see their father anymore," he said.

"Gerald isn't much of a father," she said. "He might not even notice. The boys would be sorrier to lose Melinda." She curled up against him.

"We should go right away," he said. "This place—it could make me forget who I am. And Ian, he'll just start pressuring me to take that test. I think he knows about my dreaming."

"Okay," she said. "We'll go tomorrow. Let's sleep now." She tucked herself up against him like a small animal. He put his arm over her and pulled her closer, until he could feel her heartbeat thrum against his soft side.

But he didn't let himself sleep. There was a chance that Ilford or Harriman would be looking for him, tracing him by his dreams. He ached to sleep; he'd been running for days, it seemed, and his new bulk drew him earthward. But he couldn't risk it, not until he was out of range, farther away.

Besides, he was sick of the dreaming. Of any dreaming, but especially his own. He didn't want to invade Edie's thoughts, or Melinda's, didn't want to alert Cooley to his new plans, didn't want to know how his dreams would interface with those of the dreamers who ran Vacaville.

Edie fell soundly asleep. A few minutes later Melinda crept into the room and up onto the bed beside him.

"What?" he said.

"I got scared," she said. "I couldn't sleep."

"We're going in the morning," he said.

"Good." She curled up on his other side, and the two of them slept there, tiny bodies against his mass, Edie even smaller than Melinda. There was certainly enough of him to go around.

He'd fought sleep many times before, avoiding Kellogg's dreams, but it never hurt like this, now that it was his own dreams he was avoiding, now that it mattered so much. He was tired to his core. Before long he was hallucinating, sleeping awake, and he wondered if that might not be just as bad as dreaming.

His head rolling forward, his eyes glazing, he suddenly thought, I'm as fat as Kellogg. Fatter. It was like destiny. He would be the new Kellogg. He shuddered at the thought. The horrifying prospect.

It was impossible, staying awake there under the warm bodies. He moved Melinda and Edie away from him, covered them with the blankets, and shifted his bulk out of bed. He went outside and found some cardboard boxes heaped up in the garage, took the cleanest ones and brought them inside. Careful to be quiet, he went into the kitchen and began loading supplies into the boxes: food, utensils, and pans. He began sweating immediately, and was amazed by the sensation of the sweat coursing along his new contours. He was like a world. After he filled the boxes, he moved them to the trunk of Edie's car. Packing the rest would be easy; Edie was accustomed to moving, her belongings already packed out of habit.

Finally he switched on the television, the sound low, and watched a few hours of reruns. When the sun finally came up, he went back into the bedroom and woke Edie.

"Let's go," he said.

She rubbed the sleep out of her eyes and nodded.

Everything took longer than he wanted. Roly-poly Ray was hopeless, and Dave almost as ineffectual. Still, an hour later they were nearly ready. Everett left Edie in the apartment and took Melinda down the street and around the corner, to a house where the family car was parked out of view of the front windows. Everyone was still asleep anyway. He'd found an empty gas can and a hose in the junk of the garage.

She saw what he wanted. "We should switch to one of those solar cars," she said.

"I don't know how soon we'll find one. I want to go up north from here. Edie's car is pretty low."

Melinda went to work, and soon the can was full. When Everett hauled it back around the corner, Cooley was just pulling up in his car. Edie was out of sight, probably in the house. Cooley shut off his engine, got out.

A crowd of neighbors had formed. In their bathrobes,

with uncombed hair, all of them wrong sizes and shapes and colors, with goiters and harelips and missing limbs and extra limbs. Several had summons books ready. Everett wondered if Cooley had made a round of phone calls, or gone knocking on doors, to ensure the audience.

"Welcome back, Chaos," said Cooley. "What's happening here? It's not moving day."

Cooley, who'd struck Everett as oddly broad and thick the first time he saw him, now looked more normal than anyone there. The Vacaville dreamers had succeeded. Cooley was intimidatingly gorgeous, almost heroic. Everett, ignoring him, pulled the gas can over to the side of Edie's car.

"Need some help with that? You look like you're about to have a stroke."

"Fuck you," said Everett.

The crowd oohed.

"Wait, let me guess," said Cooley. "You're angry with me." He radiated ease.

"Melinda, go inside. Cooley, say what you have to say and then leave us alone."

"You're all business, fat man." Laughter. The people surrounding them responded to Cooley like a studio audience. Or maybe just a canned laugh track.

"That's right," Everett said.

"Well, why not slow down? You look like you could use a rest. And you should take a closer look at what you're doing."

"I know what I'm doing," Everett said, and felt he'd never spoken truer words. Leaving and taking with him the people that he cared about, that's what he was doing. As he should have taken Gwen and Cale with him out of San Francisco, so long ago. He'd come close then. Chaos had come closer, oddly enough, sweeping Melinda out of Hatfork. But now Everett was going to get it right. He resolutely packed the car.

"Edie's luck is no good," said Cooley. "Neither is yours. Have you taken a good look at yourself?"

"What's standing in my way now isn't luck, Cooley. This has nothing to do with luck."

"You're headed down, friend. You've lost control of your life. You're going to hitch yourself to a woman and her two kids when you can't even take care of yourself. You take them out of this town, and they'll be helpless, completely dependent on you. All Edie knows is here. You've got your whole dream thing to cope with, which you *can't*, basically, and your luck stinks. Plus you're carrying a little weight there."

"You want to talk about luck?" said Everett. "I've got luck. The proof is, I met Edie. That was the luckiest day of my life."

He regretted the words instantly. He was letting himself be drawn into the conversation, getting defensive.

"That's sweet," said Cooley. The crowd behind him tittered. "Does she feel the same way about you? How about the day you left?"

That was enough to reactivate his anger. "Thanks for the warning," he said. "If that's all—"

"It's not all. You think I came here to see you?" He smirked. "I'm here to see Edie."

"Too bad." Everett picked up the gas can, and let a little splash onto the pavement between his feet and Cooley's. Someone shrieked. A man with a goiter and a bald woman raced to scribble out tickets.

"Don't you need that gas for your escape, big boy?" said Cooley. It was meant to be challenging, but halfway through it he met Everett's eyes, and his voice faltered.

"Don't provoke me," Everett said. "I'm tired and I'm upset. I could do anything, you know. I'm all broke up inside about my *luck*."

"Very funny," said Cooley. "But you're covering your weakness. You know you're in deep shit."

"No, I'm serious. You're the one in deep shit." He stared into Cooley's eyes. "I'm tired, like I said, and desperate. Yesterday in San Francisco I tore a house apart. You know what they say, don't you? Never fight a guy who's uglier than you, he's got nothing to lose."

"So put that gas down," said Cooley cautiously. "I like my odds."

"No thanks. I just can't spare the time." He swung the can forward and splashed gas over Cooley's pant cuffs and shoes. Cooley jumped back, too late. Everett took the can and went around to the driver's door. "I think this car has a lighter. I'd go, Cooley. Right away. Unless you want to look like you belong in this town. Do they make a version of *Playboy* for guys with no feet?"

Cooley stood, stunned. "You're dead, Chaos."

"Probably, if I stay here, you're right. But that's normal for this place. You're all dead already." He pulled out the lighter, which wasn't actually hot. It didn't matter. The sight of it sent Cooley running for his car. The chemicals in the gas were probably burning his ankles already, even unlit.

The man with the goiter braved stepping up to Everett with a summons. He was that eager, apparently, to meet his quota. He even smiled as he held out the fluttering ticket.

Everett grabbed it, and the man jumped back into the safety of the crowd. "You got the wrong guy," Everett said. "You must not have heard about the new law. Failure to live up to comic book hero standards. Cooley here is in violation." He took the ticket and followed Cooley to his car.

"What are you staring at?" he shouted at the crowd. "Write him some tickets." Cooley slammed his door shut and picked up the phone in his car. Everett slopped some more gas on the outside of Cooley's door, then stopped. He *did* need the gas. He stuffed the summons under Cooley's windshield.

Cooley started his car.

"There's your government star," Everett said. The crowd murmured and backed away. "He had to make the whole town ugly just so he could get laid." Everett took the gas back to his car. "You people ought to stuff your tickets up his goddamn beautiful ass. But you never will—"

He let it go. It wasn't their fault.

Cooley drove away. Everett got into Edie's car and sank down in the driver's seat. He replaced the lighter. He was exhausted but he wasn't trembling anymore. It was as though his fat had dissipated his anger, as though he was big enough now to absorb such feelings.

The neighbors watched dumbly as Cooley drove off, and stared at Everett in the car, and at Melinda, who was standing in the doorway.

Everett got out and waved his arms. "Go home," he said. "I don't have any replacement heroes for you. I'm just a fat slob getting out of town." As the crowd slowly dispersed, he poured the rest of the gas into the tank, then went inside and found Edie. She was packing silverware into a cigar box.

"Forget it," he said. "We'll take what's in the car. It's time to go."

Edie didn't argue. Melinda had obviously told her about Cooley's arrival.

It took five minutes to get everyone into the car, five minutes that felt like an hour. But they were near the edge of town, and they got out without being followed. Everett pushed the car up to seventy-five once they hit the highway; the overloaded station wagon complained, but he ignored it. After the first hour he eased down to sixty.

Edie helped him navigate. The map she unfolded was as big as she was. Dave had to sit sideways to accommodate his tail. For the moment they just headed north. Everett had the idea they might find the house he'd left behind, the one near the lake.

They stopped so everybody could pee behind some bushes, but ate lunch in the car. Ray and Dave were too hypnotized by the road to complain or fight. Everett knew it wouldn't stay that way for long, but after the first day it wouldn't matter so much if they stopped.

At nightfall he pulled off the highway in the middle of nowhere, onto a dirt road that led them up a hill and into some trees. He let Edie take care of giving out food. He wasn't hungry. He was dimly aware that his gruffness wasn't winning him any friends, but it didn't matter. There would be plenty of time for diplomacy later. Now he had to sleep. He went around to the back and cleared a space for himself by unloading their belongings onto the ground behind the car. Then he climbed up and curled his huge body into that space, filling it, and fell quickly and soundly asleep.

He approached the maze from the sky.

He was fat, like Kellogg. Like himself, he realized. But aloft, a blimp, an air-whale. He took his time gliding down into the corridors of the maze, and landed so gently that his feet barely stirred the dust.

He was alone where he landed, but he saw the arrows painted on the walls and followed them until he found the man lost there. It wasn't the man who had been there before. It was Ilford.

Eyes closed, his withered body held erect by the wheelchair, and snoring quietly. Around him was a litter of discarded cans and sun-bleached, rain-warped magazines.

I brought him here, Everett thought. I made good on my threat.

Nonetheless Everett stood paralyzed and silent under the pounding midday sun and stared at the man in the chair. Afraid to wake him.

Then he heard a creak and a grinding of gears behind him, around a corner of the maze. He turned.

The televangelist scuffled into view, shreds of rubber soles dragging in the dust, pamphlets spilling onto the ground. It was Cale's face that appeared on the screen.

The robot ignored Everett and approached the man in the wheelchair.

Everett cried out, "Cale!"

It didn't seem to hear. It moved behind the chair and took the handles in its corroded fingers, then tilted the chair and rolled it forward. Ilford slept on, unharmed, oblivious.

The robot pushed the wheelchair out of the fork in the maze where Everett stood and around a corner. Its manner, unmistakably, caring. Protective.

It occurred to Everett that the robot was protecting Ilford from *him*.

Now, as though something had been decided, his blimplike body rose back up out of the maze and into the glare of the sky. From above he could see the televangelist pushing the wheelchair, patiently working its way through the labyrinth.

Hovering, Everett saw another wanderer in the maze. He changed course, sailed away from the televangelist and towards the second man. Drifted down, and landed inside the walls.

The second lost man was Cooley.

Again Everett stood unseen, a bloated ghost in the corridor. Cooley had the jacket of his suit over his arm and his collar open, but he was still sweating. He turned down one path, then stopped, frowned, and stalked back to the fork. He looked up and peered intently past Everett, evidently not noticing him, instead evaluating the maze for a route of escape.

"Cooley," said Everett.

"He can't hear you," came a voice behind Everett.

He turned and saw Kellogg. The big man waddled around a corner and stood grinning.

As Kellogg had predicted, Cooley didn't respond. He wandered off, nervously peeking around corners, trying to find an exit. In a minute he was out of sight, leaving Kellogg and Everett alone.

"Well, pilgrim," said Kellogg. He took the cigar out of his mouth. "Looks like you're still a little ambivalent about gravity."

"What do you mean?"

Kellogg stepped up and poked him in the stomach. His finger passed through Everett's ghostly form. "Size but no weight," he said. "Bad recipe."

"They couldn't see me."

"Right-o."

"But I brought them here. My power is getting stronger."

"You brought us all here," agreed Kellogg. "It's your dream."

"What's supposed to happen?" said Everett.

Kellogg put the cigar back in his teeth and grimaced, making claws with his hands. "Rrrrevenge," he growled. "But you couldn't do it. You led the horse to water, cowboy."

"What?"

"You made yourself harmless, pal." Kellogg passed his hand through Everett's stomach again. "Insubstantial."

Together they floated up, twin blimps, out of the maze.

"I don't want revenge," said Everett.

Kellogg shrugged. "Whatever." He leaned back and crossed his legs, as if he were sitting on a recliner instead of bobbing in the air.

"I want to send them home."

"They'll go home. They might remember coming here, but it won't matter."

"I put Ilford in the wheelchair. I made him sick, like Cale was supposed to be."

"It'll throw a good scare into him. But it won't stick unless you want it to."

"I thought Cale would kill him."

"Yeah?" Kellogg tapped some ash off his cigar. It rained down on the maze. "Maybe you went and underestimated the strength of that father-son thing. Relations in general, Chaos. Pretty strong stuff."

"Like you and me."

"Heh. Yeah. I didn't wanna be the one to say it, for once."

"Did I ever get out of your dream? How come you know so much?"

"No more than I ever got out of yours, buddy. But that's the part you never get."

They drifted up so high now that the maze dwindled to a patch of shadow in the expanse of junkyards and highways below.

"Cooley and Ilford don't matter," said Everett, after thinking a bit. "I just had to get Edie out. I did that."

"The dame with the two brats?"

Everett nodded.

"You're getting hooked up? Chaos, the loner?"

"I guess."

Kellogg grinned. "So that's what this new gut's about," he said and reached over to pat Everett's stomach again. "You're in the family way." This time, when he patted it, Everett's fat was substantial. "Guess you're taking on some real stature after all."

Everett didn't say anything. The maze was out of sight now.

"Family's the best type of FSR," said Kellogg. "Congrats."

"FSR."

"Finite Subjective Reality, remember? No? Guess you'll always be Mr. Forget-Me-Alot."

"I remember," said Everett.

"Really? Times do change." Kellogg suddenly veered away to the right. "Well, I've got a plane to catch. See you later. Don't take any golden clocks, pal." He swam away through the clouds.

Everett was alone. He drifted, thinking, I decline revenge. I decline my power.

But there's something I should change. The family. Their bodies. Back.

He fell.

It was morning. Edie and Dave were out of the car, sitting by a small fire. Everett could hear Melinda and Ray arguing in the middle seat, but when Everett hoisted himself up, they fell silent.

Edie wasn't small anymore. And Dave's tail was gone.

Everett cantilevered his body out of the car.

"Chaos," said Edie. She came to him. "Your dream, last night. It was about us. And now look. The dream made us change back."

He didn't say anything. His head was muddled with sleep.

"Do you want some breakfast?" she asked.

He nodded. She took his arm. Melinda and Ray came out of the car. Ray was back to normal size, and Melinda didn't have fur anymore.

"Hey," said Melinda. "You're still fat."

"I guess you forgot about yourself," suggested Edie. She smiled at him shyly. "It doesn't matter."

"Well, I want my fur back," said Melinda. "That does matter."

"Sorry," said Everett.

"You jerk, you should have asked first," said Melinda.

"Melinda," said Edie.

"Well, it's true," said Melinda.

"He's doing his best. Aren't you, Chaos?"

"I'll work on it," he said. "There'll be plenty of dreams. I'll get you your fur back."

"*Tonight*," said Melinda.

"Here," said Edie. She gave him some toast with jelly and a plastic mug of tea.

"And I want my tail back," said Dave in a small voice.

"You don't want a tail," said Edie. "You just want to be like Melinda."

"No, really. I really want it back. Really."

"He liked his tail," said Melinda.

"Well, *some* of us are grateful for what you dreamed," said Edie. "Aren't we, Ray?"

"Yeah, sure," said Ray.

"So, thank you, Chaos. And thank you for trying."

"Okay," he said. "You're welcome."

———

On the road that morning, the kids busy in the back with some game, he told Edie everything he knew.

She shook her head. "What you're afraid of—it'll never happen."

"Why do you say that?"

"You'll never create some monster world, or seal yourself off in some fantasy. Because we're here. Like the way you dreamed yourself back to that place, the movie theater, but Melinda came and found you. She *remembers* it, Chaos. It was really her."

"So?"

"So we're in there with you. Inside your dreams. You let people in."

"Hey, Chaos," said Melinda from the back. "Speaking of that."

"What?" he said, meeting her eyes in the rearview.

She held out her hairless forearm and glared.

"Look," said Ray, pointing out the window on the passenger side.

"Wow," said David.

"What is that, Chaos?" said Edie.

Everett twisted his huge body and ducked his head into his shoulders to see what Ray was pointing at. Something in the sky. A flying thing, a propless helicopter, like the one Vance flew. Hard to make out in the glaring sun, but it was keeping low, matching their speed.

A troubling sight. Everett concentrated on the road.